Guns of Virtue

The brutal murder of his lawman father and the memory of a younger brother's decline into a life of lawlessness set Adam Wade on a quest for revenge on the man he holds responsible. The search takes him to the town of Virtue where the man he is hunting, rich ranch owner Hal Kember, is a pillar of society and a future state governor.

But just when he thinks his search is over and vengeance is his, Adam becomes involved in a web of deceit and murder involving Kember's beautiful wife, Laura, his errant son, Luke, and a group of stage robbers and killers. Now it will end in a shoot-out that brings one last life-changing shock for Adam.

Guns of Virtue

Peter Wilson

A Black Horse Western

ROBERT HALE · LONDON

ISBN 978-0-7090-8721-2

Robert Hale Limited
Clerkenwell House
Clerkenwell Green
London EC1R 0HT

www.halebooks.com

Typeset by
Derek Doyle & Associates, Shaw Heath
Printed and bound in Great Britain by
CPI Antony Rowe, Chippenham, Wiltshire

CHAPTER ONE

The rider dismounted on the rise above the town, patted his horse and crouched to light a slim cigar.

'This is the place,' he said, with nobody to hear except the tired chestnut.

'Virtue.' He let out a grim sigh. 'Some name for a town that's home to a man like Kember.'

He rose to his feet and stretched his aching limbs. Three days' sweat stained the armpits and back of his fading red shirt and the brim of his hat. He was a big man, tall, broad-shouldered who walked with a long stride that set him apart from the crowd.

He stared out across the wide valley below. The town had a main street of small, wooden stores and saloons, probably a sheriff's office, a hotel, barber's and blacksmith's, saddler and stable yard. And a gunsmith's. Beyond that he could make out a small church, a rail depot under construction and, in the far distance hugging the horizon, a large and impressive white house.

Virtue was a town like so many others, but with one exception as far as the broad backed rider was concerned. Virtue was the end of the line.

He tossed his half-smoked cigar aside and turned again to his horse – his only companion these last weeks.

'Tomorrow, boy. That's when we go in. Tonight we'll settle here. Tomorrow will be soon enough.'

He unsaddled the horse, slapped its rump and allowed it to stray in search of something to chew.

Adam Wade wanted more time to think about the past not the future. That he had well planned.

Elizabeth Wade was passing out the supper plates when they heard the first gunshot. She paused briefly and then realized that this was the day she had come to dread.

The streets were quiet except when the cattle-men came to town. It was a Saturday night and The Broken Spur saloon was doing a roaring trade. It had started, as always, with a few quiet drinks, hands of cards and the pianist beating out tunes for the saloon girls to sing though most of them were employed for their looks and their shapes and not their voices.

More shots were followed by drunken shrieks and the sound of shattering glass. Zachary Wade rose from his chair at the table and went to the door of the small house at the end of Main Street. Behind him his wife and two young sons stiffened as he reached for his gunbelt on the wall. Sighing, he left it hanging there.

'Leave it, Zach – they're just having fun. They'll be out of town in an hour or so—'

Wade cut a rugged figure as he stood framed by the open doorway. He tried to raise a smile in an attempt to reassure his family that this was all in a day's work and there was no need to worry.

He had been town sheriff for almost three years – ever since the family arrived at the end of the war. It had been lawless back then – deserters and gunslingers roaming the streets of Crawford Gap with the undertaker, whorehouse and saloon owners the only tradesmen making any profit.

Wade wanted something better for his wife and the boys. They had been on the move long enough, hitching a ride on a wagon train that never made it halfway across the plains.

Then he had tried earning a living of sorts as a lawman while his wife tried to make a go of a general store in a small Kansas town. It was there that his life had changed forever.

He had been on his way home from three fruit-less days' trailing a wanted bank robber when he spotted the pillar of smoke rising above the tall trees on the outskirts of town.

Irrationally he feared the worst. Why would it be his small cabin home? What about Elizabeth? The boys? He dug his spurs deep into the horse and the animal responded immediately, breaking into a gallop that took him over the rise, through the wide expanse of woodland and out into the clear-ing.

Far below was the carnage that had once been a home.

The smoke was still rising but the flames had died. Standing beside the small garden at the side of the smouldering house, her arms around the two young sons, was Elizabeth.

She turned as she heard the sound of approach-ing hoofs. Her face was smeared with the stains of her tears.

For a moment neither of them spoke, Zachary Wade's strong arms embraced his family as they all stood and watched their home slowly crumbling before their eyes.

Elizabeth and the boys had been in town when the raid happened – deserting soldiers refusing to admit the war was not going their way and·turning to wreaking havoc across the territory. The same day the Wade family had loaded up what they could salvage from the wreckage and headed wherever the road took them. They finally ended up in Crawford Gap, the small town that was to become their new home. . . .

'Don't go out there, Zach.' There was pleading in Elizabeth's voice.

'Don't worry,' he said soothingly. 'Just keep the supper warm and I'll be back before you know it.'

With that he closed the door gently behind him and stepped into the night. The Broken Spur saloon was at the other end of the town's main street but despite the poor lighting Zach Wade could see that crowds were gathering round as two drunken cowboys tested their shooting ability, and two others grappled in the dust.

The sound of breaking glass to his right caused him to spin in time to see another of the drunks crashing through the window of the barber's shop and out on to the boardwalk. His face was covered in shaving soap and he was holding an open razor in one hand and a Colt .44 in the other.

'Easy, mister,' Zach warned him, but the man didn't hear. He tumbled face down in the street, oblivious to what was going on around him. Zach smiled. It was to be hoped that the man wasn't trying to shave himself in his state – he could have succeeded in cutting his own throat. Or putting a bullet in his brain.

The lawman walked on towards the saloon, growing more worried with every step as the noise and the gunshots increased.

Up on the balcony of the local whorehouse a woman screamed.

The old wound in Zach Wade's knee started to ache but he didn't falter in his stride. He had known nights like this before but somehow he had the feeling that, if he didn't act quickly, this one could end in bloodshed. He was just about to mount the steps leading into the saloon, when a big man, dressed all in black, stepped across his path and blew cigar smoke in his direction. There was a crooked grin on the unshaven face.

'Evenin', Sheriff. Anything I can do for you?'

Zach looked the man up and down, didn't like what he saw but had no reason to cross the stranger.

'You the trail boss?'

'That's me – and this is Hal Kember's outfit.'

'Let me buy you a drink, Mr Kember – we can talk better inside.'

Zach made a move to pass the cattleman but he found his way blocked as Kember was joined by another broad-shouldered, cheroot-smoking cowhand.

'I wouldn't go in there if I were you, Sheriff,' said Kember, ice in his voice. 'My boys – they're having a bit of fun and it wouldn't be a good idea to break it up right now.'

Zach stood his ground but he knew that the cattle boss and his sidekick were itching for a fight and that his badge would offer no protection. It was time to walk away but without losing face.

All around him there was a strange silence. The two men had finished brawling in the street and the gunfire had stopped. The only sounds came from inside the saloon – a pianist hardly heard above the shouting and the screams of the females.

'Folks have to live here after you have moved on, Mr Kember. Just keep a close watch on your men. Nobody wants to spoil their fun – we just want a town to live in when you've left.'

Kember dropped his half-smoked cigar on to the step and crushed it under the heel of his boot before answering. His grinned broadly but there was no warmth there.

'Fine, Mr Lawman – now you just run along and come back at dawn. We'll give you your town back then: we'll be through with it.'

Kember turned to enter the saloon but Wade grabbed his arm.

'Listen, Kember,' – he had deliberately dropped the 'Mister' – 'any trouble and I'll hold you to blame.'

'Is that a threat, Sheriff?'

'Call it what you like, I'd say it's just a friendly warning.'

He released the cattleman's arm and turned away. Now was not the time to stand and fight. Kember was surrounded by drovers who, in their drunken state, would willingly put a bullet in him without a second thought.

As he walked slowly back towards his house at the far end of Main Street, Zach Wade could sense the cold stares on his back but he did not turn and it was not until he was closing the door and his wife had her arms wrapped around him that he could breathe easily. 'What happened, Dad?'

It was Tom, the younger of his two sons who asked the question. His father shrugged and forced a smile.

'It's like your mom said, Son – just a few cattle-men having fun. It'll pass. I spoke to the man in charge, a Mr Kember – he promised to make sure things did not get too rowdy. Now you boys, if you've finished your supper it's time for bed. We gotta start early tomorrow if you want to go on that fishin' trip.'

Once the boys had gone to their room and sure that they were out of earshot, Zach decided to confide in his wife.

'I had a word with their trail boss, a man called Kember, but I don't think that's the end of it,' he said gravely. 'I have a feeling that he's looking for trouble and didn't like the idea of being told what to do.'

Elizabeth Wade had known other nights when drifters and gangs of cattle men came to town but she had never seen her husband look so worried.

He had always been able to handle the odd rowdy drunkard, soaked in rotgut whiskey or the young kid who thought he was the fastest draw in the state. This time the frown – and did she discern a sense of fear? – told a different story.

'Maybe you should go and get help, Zach. Nathan's your deputy and there's always Charlie Mack – he's helped you out in the past.

Wade thought for a moment. Sure Nathan Barrett was his deputy but he was a young man, only married a few months and a wife expecting their first child; and Charlie – the retired sheriff who hadn't carried a gun for two years or more.

'Naw,' Zach drawled. 'Maybe I'm fretting too much – maybe they'll all calm down. . . .'

They didn't calm down.

Adam Wade couldn't sleep. He had seen the look in his father's face after he had returned from the saloon and he knew that the showdown had changed nothing. There would be more trouble ahead.

In the bunk above, his brother – at twelve years of age Tom was almost five years younger than Adam – was sleeping soundly, unaware of the occasional gunshot and shrieks of drunken laughter that shattered the night.

Pressing his face against the bedroom window, he tried to see what was happening outside. Then he heard the angry voice.

'Sheriff! Hey, Lawman! Why don't you come out here an' lock me up? Or maybe you ain't man enough? Is that it, tin star? You ain't got the guts?'

Adam could just make out the stranger who was staggering towards the house. He fired a shot into the night air. Then another.

Further down the street there was a commotion as cowboys stumbled along the boardwalks near the saloon and started to follow their drunken friend towards the house.

'All right, mister, why don't you just put down that gun and we can all get some sleep.'

The voice, calm and authoritative, was that of Adam's father. The boy had to crane his neck to see that the sheriff was now outside and had decided to confront the man.

He had just reached the gunman's side when, from around a hidden corner, a horseman rode in at full speed and with the accuracy of a man who had spent years recapturing stray cattle, roped Zach

14

Wade and dragged him to the ground.

The drunken gunman was no longer staggering. Instead, he yelled encouragement as the rider – Adam would never forget the sight of the man in the long black coat – dragged the lawman along the dusty street and into the distant darkness.

The horror of what was happening forced a scream from Adam's throat. In the bunk his young brother stirred while out in the front of the house, his mother could only look on in horror.

Briefly, the town was silent. Then, out of the darkness, the man in the black coat returned, whipping his horse into a gallop, Zach Wade being dragged along like a lump of dead meat. Drunken cowmen cheered. The man dismounted and untied the battered and bleeding lawman.

Adam could see him walking towards his mother, but, as she ran forward to attend to her husband, the stranger gripped her arm.

'When he's fit to walk, lady, tell him Kember's men don't take kindly to being told what they can do, especially by a small town nobody.'

Scoffing, he released Elizabeth's arm and strode off back towards the saloon, followed by a grinning cheering mob eager to carry on their drinking and gambling.

Adam and Tom waited until they were well out of sight before joining their mother. She was cradling her husband's head as the two boys reached her side.

It was Adam who took control. 'Come on, Ma, let's get him inside and cleaned up, it'll be fine – you'll see.'

Tom could only stand there paralysed with fear as he surveyed the bloodstained clothes of his father. The badge had been ripped from his shirt front and he wasn't even wearing his gun. He had gone out into the night unarmed to talk to the man.

Elizabeth Wade's eyes filled with tears – her voice was little more than a croak. As she turned to speak to her two sons her face told the story before the words came.

'It's no good, Son, he's dead. Your father's dead.'

The cemetery at the end of town was too small to take all the mourners at the funeral. Zachary Wade had been a popular sheriff. He had been more interested in peaceful solutions to any problems than trying to settle matters with the use of a gun.

As far as anybody could remember he had never had to use his gun – or even the threat of the gun – but, until the night of his death, he had managed to keep lawlessness off the streets of Crawford Gap. Preacher Joshua Guthrie conducted a solemn service and his words touched the hearts of many of the townsfolk. He told of the bravery of the sheriff, his honesty, his love of his family and of how the town had developed into a peaceful community under his influence.

The good citizens of Crawford Gap stood, heads bowed, tears forced back. Elizabeth Wade put her arms around the shoulders of her two young sons.

But one of them wasn't listening. Tom Wade had shed all the tears he was ever going to cry. He cared nothing for the good words of the preacher nor the well-wishes of people like deputy Nathan Barrett who kept saying how sorry he was. Even worse was the false sympathy of Jackson Leonard, the town's mayor and bank owner. Leonard had paid more visits to the house supposedly to express his condolences in the few days since the killing than he ever did out of neighbourliness while Tom's father was around.

Even a boy of twelve years had eyes to see what was on Leonard's mind. No, Tom Wade was empty of tears. All that was in his heart was hate for the man who had killed his father. Total all-consuming hate.

He turned away from his mother's comforting arm and marched out of the cemetery and up the hill at the edge of town.

Adam moved to follow, but was restrained by his mother.

'Leave him be, Son. We all have to grieve in our own way.'

The coffin was lowered into the ground; prayers were said and a temporary wooden cross bearing the name Zachary Wade and the years 1825-1868 was hammered into the ground by the undertaker. People drifted away in silence and Zach Wade became a part of the past. Up on the hillside, his younger son was filling up with even more hate. Soon he would get out of this place. He would forge his own future and it would have nothing to do with the hypocrites of a town who had watched their sheriff give his life for them. And for what? So that they could pretend he was their friend as they stood over his grave?

The fight broke out over a card game and drink. Tom Wade was losing one and had consumed too much of the other.

It was Saturday night in The Broken Spur and almost five years since the town's sheriff Zach Wade had been dragged to his death by a drunken cattle drover whose name everybody in Crawford Gap had forgotten. Everybody, that is, except the Wade family.

Widow Elizabeth, a fair-haired beauty in any one's eyes, had long since spurned the advances of Mayor Jackson Leonard and had shut herself away, coming out only to collect her needs at the general store and exchange polite conversation with other ladies in town. She had carried out her teaching duties for almost two years after Zach's death but had eventually decided that it was time to allow a younger woman – and Cissie Jordan was the perfect replacement – to take over.

Adam Wade, too, had cut himself off from friends to concentrate on his law studies and care for his mother. They occasionally showed their faces at the church or to say a prayer at the grave of the late husband and father.

A headstone bearing the legend: 'Zachary Wade – A Loving Father and Husband – Died at the Hands of the Lawless, August 15, 1868' – had replaced the wooden cross.

Tom Wade had chosen another way to handle his father's death. He had turned to drink and heavy gambling long before his time.

Instead of locking himself away and, like his elder brother, continuing his studies, Tom had decided that the world owed him something and he was going to take it.

It had taken only a few days for him to realize the futility of searching for the man who had dragged his father to his death. Cattlemen came and went through the town of Crawford Gap but the face he was searching for was never among them.

As the years passed he drank and he gambled but, because he had lost his father in the line of duty, the people of Crawford Gap suffered all his excessive behaviour in sympathetic silence.

Until one Saturday night in The Broken Spur when Sheriff Nathan Barrett decided he had seen enough.

Trouble had been brewing since early evening when Tom, freshly paid after a week's fence-mending at the JJL Ranch owned by the Leonard brothers, Jackson and Jacob, started drinking early.

Four of the town's elder citizens were enjoying a quiet hand of friendly poker when Tom staggered from the bar, brushed aside a man who was watching the game, and slumped into an empty chair.

'Don't mind if I join you fellas, do you?' he slurred.

Three of the men gave him a cold unwelcoming stare but the fourth, Cy Gallacher, proprietor and editor of the *Crawford Announcer*, smiled.

'Sit down, young Tom, you're more than welcome to join us,' he said.

His companions moved their cold stares in the direction of the newspaper proprietor but grunted their agreement.

'Sure,' one of them muttered. 'But this ain't for big bucks, young 'un.' Tom Wade straddled the empty chair but said nothing. One of the players, whom Tom knew only by sight as the owner of one of the town's two general stores, dealt the cards. His hands were shaking. He knew Tom Wade more than just by sight – he was no longer the innocent young son of Crawford's leading lawman and respected family. Fred Miller knew he was in the company of a young man who had all the makings of trouble.

The first two hands passed without incident but the winner's take was small. Then, on the third hand, Tom suddenly challenged the dealer. He reached out, gripped the man's wrist and held his arm firmly against the table.

'You holdin' back on me, mister?' The voice was slurred, the long bout of drinking starting to have its effect.

The man stuttered a reply that only increased Tom's rising anger. 'Take it easy, I'm holding nothing back, young feller—'

Tom tightened his grip.

'Don't call me young feller – and let's see what you're holding.'

Cy Gallacher decided to join in. 'Look, Tom, Fred doesn't cheat and if you don't like the way we play, well, nobody invited you to join us.

'Why don't you just leave? Take your money and go—'

Tom rose to his feet but he was stopped by a

heavy hand on his shoulder.

'That's good advice, Tom, I'd take it if I were you.'

Nathan Barrett was grim-faced as Tom turned to face the man who had followed his father into the sheriff's office at Crawford Gap. Shaking himself free he stared at the other men at the table and then at his one-time friend Nathan.

He put on his hat and stormed out into the street, cursing as he left the saloon. Barrett watched him go but he knew for certain that there would be more trouble from Tom Wade before he was much older. . . .

Fred Miller never saw the man who hit him. He was attacked from behind as he turned to lock up the store for the night, sent into unconsciousness by a violent blow to the back of the head, probably from a gun butt. When he came to, he struggled to his feet and surveyed the store. Provisions were scattered across the floor, the safe door was open and the contents gone.

The pain from the crack he had received to his skull was excruciating and when Sheriff Barrett asked him if he could tell him anything that might help to track down the thief, all he could recall was, 'I didn't see him, Nat, and the only thing I remember was the smell of stale whiskey.'

It was the night that 17-year-old Tom Wade rode out of Crawford Gap for the last time.

Six years after her husband was killed and more than a year since she saw her younger son Tom for the last time, Elizabeth Wade was struck down by a fever. At first she thought it would pass and ordered Adam not to fuss so much. After two days and no signs of any improvement – if anything the fever was getting worse – he called in the doctor.

'Keep her warm, give her plenty of water and I'll call again tomorrow,' he told Adam.

He did call again the next day only to find that Elizabeth had passed away in the night. Adam was staring silently at his feet as he sat hunched on the porch. In six short years he had lost both his parents and his younger brother whose face he had last seen on a Wanted poster. He had managed to keep that away from his mother. The people of Crawford Gap were full of sympathy at the funeral – Elizabeth was buried alongside her husband and the Reverend Joshua Guthrie was glowing in his tribute to 'one of the finest ladies the town had ever known'.

As the mourners filed away from the small cemetery, Cy Gallacher, owner editor of the *Crawford Announcer*, caught up with Adam.

'I know this is a bad time for you, lad, but your mother was well liked in town and around the county. I'd like it if you would let me write a tribute in this week's edition.'

'Sure, Cy, that would be nice,' said Adam quietly. 'If there's anything I can do—'

'There is, Adam. If you have a picture of your mother that I could use to include in the newspaper I could—'

Adam interrupted him. 'I think I can arrange that. I'll call in at the office later, if that's all right.'

Gallacher thanked him and moved on, leaving Adam alone in the street to fight back the tears as he turned and headed for the house, deep in thought.

Maybe now was the time to move on. His father and mother were in the ground; his young brother, still only eighteen years old, was an outlaw on the run, wanted for armed bank robbery and wounding. And although nobody in Crawford Gap had ever raised the subject in public, Adam knew that his brother was the person everybody felt was responsible for the break-in and assault at the general store the night he left town.

He took down the picture of his mother from its pride of place above the fire. She stood tall in a typical side-on pose, head held high with her face turned towards the camera over her left shoulder, arms folded, hair tied back, but only the hint of a smile. A picture of dignity.

Adam clearly remembered the day the photograph had been taken. The occasion was to celebrate the completion of a new classroom at the school where she was the teacher. It had been Elizabeth Wade's endless cajoling and encouraging that had persuaded the local fathers to carry out the work, repair the storm damage done to the creaking old building.

That was nearly seven years ago when his father was still sheriff of Crawford Gap and he and brother Tom were just starting to face up to the fact that one day they would be leaving home to make their own way in the world.

Adam removed the photograph from its frame, slid it into his pocket and headed for the office of the *Crawford Announcer* and the moment that was to determine the rest of his life.

Cy Gallacher was leaning over a bench of metal type which he was meticulously arranging into the front page headline of that week's newspaper when Adam entered the office.

Apart from Cy there was an old grey-haired man – whom Adam believed was Charlie Ricketts who had started the paper several years earlier – sitting at a table studying a pile of old editorials. Adam took the photograph of his mother and handed it to the newspaper owner.

'That's kind of you, Adam. Your mother was a fine woman. I'll try to get that across in her obituary piece. If there's anything you want me to put in, I—'

But Adam wasn't listening. Instead he was staring at the row of type that Cy was arranging as the head-line for the next edition.

Although the type was upside down and back to front there was no mistaking its annoncement. Adam ran around the bench to make sure that what he saw was the truth.

It was there. And with it a photograph of the man himself.

HAL KEMBER RUNS FOR CONGRESS
RANCH OWNER EXPECTS TO WIN IN CLOSE VOTE

Cy stopped what he was doing and stared at Adam. The younger man's face was ashen, as though he had seen a ghost.

'What's wrong, Adam?'

Adam pointed at the type ready to be turned into a newspaper headline.

'This. This story. Where's it from, Cy?'

The editor looked puzzled.

'I don't understand, Adam, what—?'

'Where's this story come from?'

'It's on the wires. We take stories from all over the state, Adam, you know that. We couldn't keep the paper going with what's happening here in Crawford Gap.'

Adam wasn't listening. Instead, he was staring at the photograph that was with the newspaper story. Did he recognize the face? He stared harder. He wasn't sure. Could it be . . . was it?

'What is it, Adam?

Adam Wade tried to control his emotions.

'Just tell me, Cy. Tell me about the story.'

Gallacher visibly relaxed. 'Like I said, it came over on the wires. It's a story about the election for Congress and I thought it might interest local folk to know who their man is in the government these days. Kember's hoping for a seat in Congress. Why are you so het up about it?'

Adam Wade tried to gather his thoughts as his mind raced back to the night that his father was dragged through the streets to his death by a man in a long, black coat.

He remembered the name. And, as he stared at the grainy photograph with the story that was to go at the top of the front page of the next edition of the *Crawford Announcer*, he was sure he remembered the face.

When he spoke, the words were quietly delivered.

'Cy, I want you to write nice words about my mother. I know you'll do that. But I may not be here to read them.'

The bewildered newspaperman waited for further explanation, but when it came he wished he hadn't.

'Six years ago, Cy, before you bought the paper from Charlie over there, my father was killed by a cattleman who had had too much to drink. He dragged my father through the streets to prove a point to his men . . . that he was the boss and no small-town sheriff was going to tell him what to do. I saw it, Cy – with my own eyes. That killer was the man who aims to be our new state congressman, Hal Kember.'

Gallacher gasped and Charlie looked up from his papers.

'Adam, there must be some mistake. Hal Kember's a respectable rancher outside of Virtue. He's the mayor of the town and has poured money into the place and turned it into a thriving little town. It can't be the same man, Adam. There must be some mistake.'

Adam Wade stared coldly at the newspaperman.

'Yeah, there's been a mistake, Cy, and Hal Kember made it by showing his face again.'

He turned and walked out of the newspaper office and headed back to his house. There he packed his guns, his saddle-bag and a few provisions to keep him going until he reached the town of Virtue.

*

Adam woke early on the tenth day of his ride out of Crawford Gap – and now he was on the last steps of the journey to avenge the death of his father. He threw the saddle over his horse's back, mopped his brow and mounted up. The time had come to seek out his father's killer.

CHAPTER TWO

Cy Gallacher was right. Virtue was a thriving little town. It was early morning when Adam dismounted at the blacksmith's and livery yard that marked the entrance to the main street. He paid for feed and corraling for his horse, giving the young man an extra dollar for special treatment and then set off in search of a hotel or rooming-house.

Like every stranger who passed through towns like Virtue, he attracted some attention from the locals as they went about their morning business. A few nodded in his direction, one even stopped and was about to speak but then realized he did not know the tall, dark man in the red shirt after all and passed along without a word.

A group of children were being ushered into a small schoolroom by a harassed schoolmistress, and the owner of the first general store he came to was busy helping to unload a supply wagon. A stage with six tired horses stood near a small office beside a saloon. It was then that Adam saw the name for the first time. In large bold letters across the balcony above the batwings were the words: KEMBER'S HOTEL & SALOON.

He allowed himself a humourless smile. If he guessed right it would be the only place in town to offer accommodation. The Kember he remembered would not have encouraged competition. He stepped up on to the boardwalk and entered the hotel.

The room – complete with its piano, stage, card tables and bar that stretched along one side – was deserted except for an old man who was cleaning the floors and tables. He looked up from his bucket as Adam entered.

'Ain't nobody here yet, mister.'

Adam smiled. 'I can see that, old feller. Except I don't think you are nobody. Where can I go to rent a room?'

The man stopped sweeping the floor and took his time looking the newcomer up and down. He obviously liked what he saw.

'Well now, you could try going through that door over there – I'm sure the lady will take care of you.'

'Lady?'

The old man chuckled.

'Sure, mister. None better.'

That was all Adam got out of the old man as he returned to his cleaning duties so he made his way across the room towards the door the man had pointed out.

He tapped lightly on the door and pushed it open to reveal a small office. In the far corner was a woman immersed in a large red ledger-style book that was spread across the desk.

She stopped writing and looked up as Adam entered. Her smile was friendly, though for some reason Adam had the feeling that she did not get the opportunity to use it very often. He guessed that being stuck behind the desk in the back room of a hotel-saloon in a small Texas town would not be the life she would have placed at the top of her wish list.

Adam removed his hat and felt himself strangely unsure as the woman rose from behind the desk and came towards him.

She was tall and despite the disguise of a bustle and high-collared white shirt she was wearing, she was slender and narrow-waisted. Her black hair was pinned back from her rounded face. But her skin was pale – she spent little time outdoors. Adam guessed she was scarcely much older than himself.

'Are you looking for a room, Mr—?'

The voice was soft and welcoming. The smile even more so.

'Wade, Adam Wade, and yes, I'd like a room for

the next few days.'

'We've got one at the top of the stairs. It needs cleaning – I'll get old Jake to see to it. We don't get many visitors here in Virtue.'

'Seems like a nice little town,' said Adam, following the woman up the stairs.

She said nothing, but Adam got the distinct impression that she didn't entirely agree with his opinion of Virtue.

She unlocked the room, handed him the key and left him alone to his thoughts. He stood at the bedroom window and stared out at the quiet street below, at the sheriff's office and jail, the Diamond Saloon, the barber's shop, two restaurants and a general store on the opposite side, and thought over his next move. Ever since the night his father had been dragged to his death through the streets of Crawford Gap more than six years ago he had promised he would get even with the cold-blooded killer who had robbed him and his brother of a father. Hal Kember was that man – he was sure. Almost sure.

But what did that mean now? Would he – could he – search him out before gunning him down in cold blood? Adam didn't know – but what was the alternative? Take him in and force him to stand trial for a murder committed so many years ago?

People moved on. Times changed, memories

faded. Who in Crawford Gap would remember that night clearly enough to point the finger at a man who was planning to be elected a congressman? Would any of them even thank him for bringing his father's killer back to face justice, raking up bad old times.

Adam smiled at the idea, but in truth he had no opinion. For six years he had thought of this moment, the day when he could reach out and almost touch his father's killer. But he was no cold-blooded butcher and he could not turn into one, even to avenge the death of his father. For the past five years Adam Wade had been a sworn-in United States deputy marshal.

The sun was high in the clear blue sky and the small town of Virtue was basking in the heat and enjoying a quiet afternoon. Except in the bar of the Diamond Saloon. There, the heat was being generated not by the sun but by a game of poker.

Four men of varying size, age and appearance sat huddled over a corner table near the piano. In the centre of the table was a pile of coins and dollar bills.

The oldest of the four players emptied his whiskey glass, took his time to scrutinize the faces of the other three and then, with a sigh of resignation, threw in his cards.

The man to his left, a thin-faced cadaverous figure known around Virtue as Doc, though nobody knew whether he had studied medicine, puffed heavily on a thin cigar before deciding that he, too, was out of the game and stacked his hand.

That left just two – a thickset, bearded cowhand wearing a permanent scowl and opposite him a fresh-faced young man barely twenty years old.

The younger player leaned back in his chair and waited as the cowhand moved his cards, showing the first signs of nerves.

The rest of the room was silent as even the barman stopped polishing his glasses to await the outcome.

'I think you're bluffin', kid,' said the older man.

'It'll cost you to find out, mister,' the younger man said, a sneer in his voice.

There was a tense silence as the two men stared across the table, but it was eventually broken when the cowhand picked up a handful of coins and bills and threw them onto the table.

'Right, boy, let's see what you got.'

The young man leaned forward and slowly laid his cards on the table . . . four kings and an ace.

The cowhand cursed. The kid smiled. The others backed away. There was trouble in the air – no hard-nosed cowboy liked to be shown up by some fresh-faced kid. Even this one.

The young man leaned across the table and started to scoop up his prize money, but before he could do so his opponent rammed his hand hard down in the younger man's wrist.

'We ain't through here, sonny. You palmed those cards.'

'Oh, I think we are through, mister,' said the other and before the older man could move, the kid swung a fist that caught his rival across the jaw, sending him crashing against the saloon wall.

Immediately the cowboy reached for his gun but he was too slow. The kid was on top of him in an instant, his flying boot catching the man's gun hand. He let out a piercing shriek as the pain ripped through his arm and before he had time to move the young man had wrestled the revolver from his grip and thrown it across the room.

Then he stood over the stricken cowboy.

'You're lucky I'm in a good mood, mister. You're too old to be picking fights. It was your call and I beat you fair and square. Learn to live with it.'

With that he turned, scooped up his winnings and walked slowly out of the saloon.

Adam Wade had washed and shaved away the remnants of his beard and was idling away the early afternoon staring out of his hotel room when he saw a young man leave the saloon across the street.

He had a spring in his step, as though he had just enjoyed success at the card table or with one of the girls in the back rooms.

Adam remembered the days back in Crawford Gap when he had discovered the same feeling. He was about to turn away when the doors of the saloon burst open and a bearded cowboy staggered out on to the sidewalk. The man had clearly indulged in too much of the gut-rot liquor that saloons like the Diamond passed off as whiskey. Adam watched as the man staggered out into the middle of the street and yelled at the younger man who was walking towards the general store. Adam could not make out what was being shouted but the cowboy suddenly drew his gun and fired in the general direction of the other.

The rest of the street was deserted.

What happened next took no more than an instant.

As the younger man to turned to face him, the drunken card player took aim. But before he could squeeze the trigger, Adam acted. Swinging from the window ledge of his hotel room he hurled himself from the balcony. Before the drunken gunman could fire again, Adam had sent him crashing to the dusty street, sending his gun spinning out of reach. The man let out a yell as he crashed under the weight of the stranger.

Adam hauled the other man to his feet, kicked

the fallen gun well out of reach and then, with a single punch, sent the man staggering backwards towards the boardwalk.

He made no move to get up, instead wiping the blood from his broken nose while Adam retrieved the gun and hurled it into a nearby horse trough.

'You ought to be more careful who you turn your back on, son,' Adam said, as the young man approached.

The kid didn't smile or offer his thanks. Instead he just looked down at the man sprawled in the street.

'Hackett's just a bad loser, mister, said I cheated him,' he said. 'Anyways he couldn't have hit the side of a house from that distance. Not in his state.'

'Nice to know that, now,' said Adam. 'Maybe I should've just let him try.'

He turned to walk away but the young man gripped his arm.

'No – sorry. You weren't to know. Er, thanks. I owe you. 'Sides, you're a stranger in town, ain't you?'

'Just got in. Name's Adam Wade.'

'Luke,' said the kid, stretching out his hand. Adam took it firmly.

The lad had a strong, confident grip.

'Did you?' Adam asked, when he had released the other's hand.

'Huh?'

'Did you cheat him? That man, Hackett.'

Suddenly the young man broke into a grin. 'Now that's between me and him, ain't it? No concern of a stranger in town.'

Adam returned the smile. 'Suppose not. It's that I'd like to know I hadn't just saved a card sharp from getting blown to Kingdom come.' He turned and left the younger man standing in the middle of the street and headed for the sheriff's office where he had official business.

Jack Naylor, long-serving sheriff of Virtue, reminded Adam of his own father. Broad-shouldered with greying untidy hair and thick moustache, Naylor filled his checked shirt almost to button-bursting and he also walked with a slight stoop. But there any resemblance to the late Zachary Wade ended – Naylor clearly believed in the law of the gun. Even in his office he wore a six-shooter, slung low across his hip. But he appeared to be a friendly sort and when Adam introduced himself as a deputy US marshal there was more than a flicker of interest in the local lawman's face.

'And what's a federal law officer doing in these parts?' he asked, offering Adam a chair across from his own seat by his desk. 'Don't tell me there's some bad guy on the run here in Virtue that I don't know 'bout?'

Adam knew he had to be careful how he answered that and offered a smile in return.

'No, nothing like that. I was just passing though and I noticed that you had a hotel called Kember. That wouldn't belong to Hal Kember, would it? The rancher who's planning to be a congressman?'

'Sure would, Marshal,' beamed the sheriff, clearly relieved that the stranger in town was not on some official business that would bring him any trouble. 'Why do you want to know?'

'I think Kember was an old friend of my father's. I was planning on dropping in with my regards and I thought you might let me know where I can find him.'

Naylor rose from his chair and walked around his desk. His friendly grin encouraged Adam.

'Look, Marshal, there's not a body in Virtue who doesn't know where you can find Hal Kember. He owns the Big K a few miles outside town. A smart white house with a red roof.

'He's the town mayor and it's because of him that this town is a peaceful, easy-going sort of place. That makes my job easy. Precious little gun play; maybe a drunk or two.'

'Like Hackett?' Adam interrupted with a smile.

'Cabe Hackett? You've met him?'

Adam related the tale of what had happened only minutes before he had called on the sheriff.

'He was ready to gun down some kid until I . . . let's say I interrupted him.'

Naylor frowned. 'That's not like Hackett. He's a big drinker and spends half his day ranting about nothing in particular but he's no hot shot with a gun. He must have been real mad.'

'And drunk,' Adam offered helpfully. 'Now he's got a real sore head.'

'Don't suppose it'll hurt him none,' Naylor said from his position perched on the corner of his desk. 'Who was the kid?'

'Luke something. Didn't catch his other name.'

Naylor smiled.

'You can count yourself among the good guys. Sounds to me like you'd be made real welcome at the Big K.'

'How come?'

'Like I said, Hal Kember likes to keep a quiet town. He'll like it even more to know that you saved his wayward son from a bullet. That'd have been Luke Kember who got Hackett all riled up. No doubt over a game of cards.'

Adam stood and they shook hands again as he prepared to leave. It was still early in the afternoon and he had not yet figured out his best approach to visit the Big K and his showdown with the man who had killed his father. It was six years since that fateful night in Crawford Gap and a man like Kember

41

could have conveniently forgotten it. Perhaps he would tell him that he had just saved his son from a bullet in the back. That might get his attention.

He was about to leave the sheriff's office when there was a commotion outside and a man burst in breathlessly.

The sun was high in a clear sky as the three riders waited and watched the cloud of dust come slowly closer. They re-checked their guns; not a word passed between them; they had done all the talking and planning. They knew the routine and they knew that, if it came to gun play, they were ready.

The stage appeared briefly from behind a row of rocks but soon disappeared again, its progress only visible because of the rising dust from the trail.

The minutes passed until, at a signal from the gunman on the pinto, the trio raised their bandannas to cover the lower half of their faces, and kicked their horses into action.

The Virtue-bound coach swung around a sharp bend in the road as the raiders reached the gap at the bottom of the hill.

The lead rider, in black shirt and black stetson, fired into the air and ordered the stage driver to stop.

Instead, the man with the reins lashed the lead horses into a gallop and the older man riding shotgun raised his rifle.

It was a fatal error. The second of the masked men didn't hesitate; his aim was true as the bullet from the six-gun tore into the shotgun rider's chest.

He slumped sideways, forcing the driver to struggle with the reins to keep the horses on the road and the stage on its wheels. But, as he reined in the team, there was another shot – this time from inside the coach. The third rider, the youngest of the three, let out a yell and grasped his chest, spinning from his saddle and hitting the dust with a body-jarring thud.

Slowly, he staggered to his feet and, in blind fury, fired recklessly at the side window of the coach. He emptied his gun, screamed a curse and then dropped to his knees as the pain from his wound became excrucing.

'Throw down the strong-box!' yelled Black Shirt, dismounting and keeping his gun aimed at the chest of the driver, who abandoned any idea of reaching for his own rifle.

'Jess, take a look inside,' he ordered.

Jess helped his stricken partner to his feet and edged towards the coach door, his six-gun levelled at the open window.

Inside, one passenger lay slumped in his seat, his sightless eyes staring at nothing; another cringed in the far corner while the third – a young woman –

sobbed uncontrollably.

Quickly two of the outlaws relieved the passengers of their money and released one of the lead horses and strapped the heavy strong box across the animal's back. Jess helped his wounded friend back into the saddle and the three headed back into the hills.

The man in black – clearly the gang's leader – had barked an order to the stage driver. The message was clear and the man had climbed down from his lofty seat to carry out the order to release the five remaining horses and send them scattering to the hills. By the time the old man had rounded them up the trio would be long gone.

Once out of sight, the men lowered their masks and paused for rest. Things had not gone to plan.

'Is it bad, kid?' Black Shirt enquired of the injured rider who nodded.

'I'm hurting, Sam. Real bad.'

Sam thought for a moment. The kid needed a doctor, but they could hardly ride into town and pay a visit to the nearest sawbones. But what were his options? He liked the kid, but did he like him enough to take a chance on him? Maybe not.

He knew all about the ranch nearby. If he could get the kid there, he knew he could persuade the rancher to bring out the local doc to see to the kid's wound.

But first they would have to find a hiding place for the strong box.

Sam cursed the kid for getting himself shot. What should have been a simple stage hold-up had ended in two pointless deaths.

Now he had the added burdens of a wounded friend and the prospect of leaving their cache hidden until it was safe to return to collect it.

Briefly he considered the other alternative – a bullet to the head of the injured kid who had killed the passenger. But he dismissed that almost immediately. That was not how Sam Brock did business. And he also knew that there was refuge to be found at the nearest ranch house. He had made sure of that as part of the planning for this stage robbery. It was always best to have a back-up plan if things went wrong. Like now.

The main street of Virtue became a seething mass of bodies as the stage drew to a halt outside the sheriff's office. Townsfolk rushed forward at the sight of the shotgun rider slumped in his seat. The driver climbed down and hurried inside with his story.

The sheriff had company – a tall, broad-shouldered stranger who looked like he could be another lawman.

Breathlessly, the man blurted out his garbled report of the hold-up.

'We wuz only a few miles outa town when they hit us. They got Brett and one of the passengers. They got away with the strongbox and—'

'Strongbox?' the sheriff interrupted, surprised.

'We wuz carrying it to the bank. It wuz the payroll for the men working on the new railroad up north. Nobody wuz s'posed to know what we were carryin'. And whatever else they could take.' He paused for breath but then went on hurriedly, 'There wuz three of 'em, Sheriff, but we got one – leastways winged him, before they done for Brett,' said the old man enthusiastically. 'Don't reckon he'll get far without being patched up.'

It was then that Adam Wade spoke. 'Did you get a look at any of them?'

'No, they wore bandannas. One was all in black; rode a pinto. But, like I said, one of them's carrying a bullet in his chest, or maybe his shoulder, and I heard one of 'em say the name Jess. Get a posse together, Sheriff. Shouldn't take long to root 'em out.'

Sheriff Naylor was less than enthusiastic about forming a posse. He had tried that in the past and they never amounted to much more than a load of gun-happy drunks from the saloon looking for blood.

'Hold it, Ned. We can't just go chasing around the countryside like a mob looking for a lynching,'

46

he said calmly. 'Just leave it to us. You get along, get the doc out to see to those folk in the stage. He'll call the undertaker for Brett and the passenger. Any others hurt?'

'Naw, young girl blubbing her eyes out and some guy wettin' hisself but they'll live,' he scoffed.

Naylor nodded. 'Right, Ned. I'll shift that crowd that's gathering out there. Get them to go about their business. This is a job for the law.'

The old man shuffled out and the sheriff and Adam discussed their next move.

'Looks like you'll have to put off your visit to see Hal Kember for a while, Marshal. I'll need you around here.'

Adam thought about that. He was out of his territory on a mission that was anything but lawful and now he was being asked to join a search for a group of stage robbers and killers. Yes, Hal Kember could wait. But he kept this and his other thoughts to himself . . . especially about the notion that somebody knew that strongbox was on board what was a regular passenger stage. And that somebody had passed on the knowledge to three grateful outlaws.

CHAPTER THREE

Sam Brock leaned back and ordered the others to halt. The wounded rider was slumped in his saddle and Jess had made it plain that they should move on and leave the kid to fend for himself. Brock thought about that, leave the kid with his share of the payroll money and head for the border. Getting shot was a risk they took in their line of business. If it happened, it happened. But he had dismissed the thought. He might need the kid in future and getting him patched up would not be a problem. He would call in a favour. He stopped at the top of the rise and gazed out across the valley to the ranch house in the distance. It had changed for the worse since his last visit. Even from this distance he could make out the blistered and peeling paintwork, the broken fence of what had been a corral, the rundown appearance of the main house.

But appearances mattered little to Brock. He

knew it was a safe place to hole up while the kid's wound healed.

'You sure about this, Sam?' said Jess uncertainly, as he followed the man in black down the slope towards the ranch.

'I'm sure. Duggan and me go back a long way. It'll be fine.'

He was sure of that. Duggan might be spending his latter years as a small-time farmer but it wasn't always that way. The two men had ridden with the grey coats during the war ... afterwards Duggan had been his trail boss through a number of cattle drives.

They had drunk hard and fought hard side by side down the years. There had been times when they had shared a jail cell in some small town following a night of drunkenness or saloon bar brawling.

There had been a sort of unspoken alliance between the pair, but then Duggan had suddenly gone all law-abiding and respectable, leaving Brock to roam the state and earn his living outside the law.

Joe Duggan's ranch was about to become a refuge for three men on the run.

Long hours in the hot sun produced no results for Adam and Sheriff Naylor in their search for the fugitives and the pair returned to Virtue believing that the stage robbers could already have made their getaway across the border.

Both men were tired and low in spirits after their fruitless search.

'We could try again come daylight,' Naylor suggested, as they dismounted outside his office. 'They won't be making good time with a wounded man holding them back.'

Adam wasn't so sure. He didn't know the county, but had seen enough of it to realize that there were trails leading in all directions. They could be anywhere but he agreed to meet the following morning.

It was late when he left the sheriff's office and was heading back to his room, but a change of mind took him instead to the hotel's quiet bar room.

Adam had never been a heavy drinker but tonight he felt that a couple of beers would help him sleep. One way or another tomorrow was going to be a busy day, not least because he had decided that, whatever Naylor had planned, he would be paying his visit to Hal Kember. He was sitting alone at a corner table, nursing his beer and thinking about his plans for the following day, when his thoughts were interrupted by a female voice.

'Mr Wade, isn't it?'

He looked up from his drink and into the face of the woman he recognized as the one who had welcomed him to the hotel that morning. He stood

up, took off his hat and smiled. 'That's right, miss—'
She had changed from her high-necked white shirt
and bustled dress and was now wearing an outfit of
green blouse and brown calf-length skirt.

'Mrs,' she corrected him, sliding into a chair
opposite. 'But most people around these parts call
me Laura.'

Adam had never felt completely comfortable in
the company of women – other than his mother –
but instinctively he had the idea that Laura could be
different. She made him feel at ease and her smile
was genuine. His few experiences with the opposite
sex had been short, occasionally sweet, but always
less than memorable. Maybe this time things would
improve.

Even the first time – her name was Lily he
remembered and she was a saloon singer – was a big
disappointment in his education and ever since, he
had felt that he lacked the emotion to match the
occasion. But, as Laura settled opposite him, he felt
he was meeting somebody who could change all
that.

He even noticed that her left hand was ringless. A
widow, he assumed.

'Bad business today,' she said. 'The stage hold-up
and the shootings.'

Adam nodded agreement. 'Bad business.'

She looked him up and down before observing, 'I

hear you're a lawman.'

He returned her smile. 'Of sorts. Deputy US Marshal.'

'And what's a deputy US marshal doing here in a quiet little town like Virtue?'

Adam took a sip of his beer and thought for a moment.

Should he tell her? Should he let her in on the reason for his presence in her 'quiet little town'?

He could give her the horrific details of the night he watched helplessly as his father was dragged through the streets to his death; how his mother's broken heart had become a broken spirit; how his brother had changed from a loving son to an outlaw on the run following his father's murder.

He could also tell her how more than six years of bitterness and thought of revenge had come to a head in the office of the *Crawford Announcer* less than two weeks ago.

Instead, he said simply, 'It's personal.'

She gave him a strange inquisitive look but didn't press him on the subject. There would be time enough for that later. Afterwards. . . . Adam ordered a third beer and they sat and talked of other things until finally Laura said provocatively, 'Well, Mr Adam Wade, we could sit here all night talking about nothing in particular but I think there are better things we could do with our time, don't you?'

Adam finished his drink, looked around the room to find that the others were far too interested in their cards to notice the couple climbing the stairs to the rooms above.

All except one. Luke Kember had seen it all and allowed himself a smug smile that had nothing to do with the three kings and two aces that he held in his hand. Here was more information that would come in useful when the time came.

Adam stirred early the following morning to find that Laura had already left. He washed and shaved quickly and was looking forward to a hearty breakfast before joining the sheriff. He would give over one more day of his time in the search for the stage robbers and after that Naylor was on his own – apart from any help he could raise from the good citizens of Virtue. If this was like any other town he had known – and in particular Crawford Gap – that would amount to nothing much more than fine words and good wishes.

It would, in their view, be up to the law and stage company to hunt down the killers. It was not the job of simple, hard-working souls who only wanted to go about their daily business.

Dressed and washed, he was descending the staircase when he heard raised voices coming from somewhere below.

One he recognized: it belonged to Laura. The other – a man's – was vaguely familiar, but he couldn't put a name or a face to it.

They were having a heated discussion and although he was unable to make out what they were saying he did catch two words clearly: Adam Wade.

He increased his pace and hurried down in the direction of the argument. As he stepped into the doorway of what appeared to be a small eating area, the pair froze. There was a sudden uncomfortable silence. Adam instantly recognized the man: it was Luke Kember, the young card player whom he had saved from a bullet the previous day. The young man turned towards him, a self-satisfied smirk on his face.

'Ah, the man himself. Our visiting marshal.' There was a note of derision in his voice.

Adam was baffled. 'What's going on?'

Luke Kember walked towards him, keeping the smug smile.

'I was just telling Laura here; I called in to give you some good advice, mister, to sort of repay you for that favour you did me yesterday. You remember?'

'Sure do, son. If I hadn't you might not be here to tell the story. So, what's this advice you're offering?'

'Well now, Marshal, I don't know what your business here in Virtue might be, but my advice is that you get it done real quick and head back the way you came.'

Adam did not like the young man's attitude, but he thought it best to play along. 'Tell me, kid, why is that such good advice?'

Luke Kember turned to face Laura and then back to Adam. He was grinning more widely now, like it was his moment of triumph.

'Let's just say I wouldn't give much for your future once the news gets out that you've been sleeping with the wife of Hal Kember.'

CHAPTER FOUR

Young Luke Kember brushed Adam aside and strode out of the hotel with such a purpose that his next stop would be the Big K ranch with the information that would have Adam either run out of town or shot down in the middle of the main street. Either way, Adam had tasted the forbidden fruit and he would be expected to pay for the pleasure.

Laura could see his concern – she knew instinctively that it wasn't fear – in the face of the man who had made love to her the previous night. Not expertly, she had to admit, but with more practice . . . who knew? She was now dressed in the high-collared shirt and bustled skirt she had been wearing when he first saw her. She was once again the businesswoman running Virtue's only hotel.

'Don't worry, Adam, Luke won't tell his father. He'll just keep the information to get more money out of me whenever he can't pay his gambling debts.'

Adam was astonished. 'Your own son is black-mailing you?'

She laughed at the idea. 'Hey, I'm not that old. Luke's my stepson. I'm the second Mrs Hal Kember and Luke's the second coming of his father. My husband is used to getting what he wants. His son's the same. But you don't have to worry about him.'

He studied Laura closely. No doubt it wasn't the first time she had strayed from the marriage bed and he knew he wouldn't be the last to enjoy her talents and charms.

She was a good-looking woman – better judges than Adam might even have classed her as beautiful – and he wondered how she had managed to tie herself to a man she clearly had little affection for and, if he remembered last night correctly, cared little about what people said of her.

She must have been reading his thoughts.

'Hal's a lot older than me and I've got my folks to thank me for – well, for all this.' She spread her arms.

'This hotel? It's yours?'

'As long as I'm seen to be the good, dutiful wife of my father's friend and fellow cattleman.'

'Who's now running for Congress.'

She chuckled.

'Our very own man in the state capital,' she laughed. 'Which is one of the reasons I have to be seen to be on my best behaviour and why Luke won't be opening his big mouth about last night.'

She stretched up and kissed Adam full on the mouth.

'Now,' she said, suddenly changing the subject, 'what can I cook up for breakfast? I think you've earned it after your, er, exertions last night.' As she walked off to what Adam assumed was the hotel kitchen he had the uneasy feeling that, even if he wanted to back away from his planned showdown with Hal Kember, the fates were conspiring against him. And Laura Kember would be part of those fates.

They rode the trail south-west out of town, stopping at the occasional smallholding to ask if anybody had spotted three riders – one of them wounded – heading towards the border. Nobody had.

'They're long gone, Sheriff,' Adam suggested, deep into the afternoon. 'They will be well across the state border now. We can't hope to track them down.'

Naylor was reluctant to call it a day.

'They may have gone west,' he argued. 'And if they did . . . well, they could be holed up in any one of six or seven places.'

'And what chance have we got of picking the right one?' Adam argued.

Naylor looked downcast. Wade was right: the stage robbers had gone by now and reluctantly he had to admit defeat in their search. Night was falling and they had spent a long day in the saddle. It was time to head back to town and explain to the good folk of Virtue that, without the help of a posse, there was no hope of bringing the killers to justice.

At the moment the two lawmen were turning their mounts towards the distant outskirts of the town, two other riders were dismounting outside a neat white picket fenced house at the heart of Virtue's residential district.

There were two riders, but three horses.

One was Sam Brock, the other a younger, meaner-looking man was Jess – he was merely there as back-up and as Brock knew, useful with a gun if he was needed – and they were outside the little house that was the home of Doc McLaine, the town's only medical man.

'Stay here and keep your eyes open,' Brock ordered, as he opened the gate and headed for the house. He tapped lightly on the door – he wanted no prying eyes from neighbours' twitching lace curtains to witness the visit – and waited.

A sour-faced, middle-aged woman opened the

door and glared at him.

Brock tried the polite approach, raised his hat and smiled. 'Sorry to trouble you, ma'am, but is the doc at home?'

Before she could answer a voice came from inside the house. 'Who is it, Martha?'

Brock widened his smile. 'I guess that means the answer is yes,' he said.

'You'd better come inside,' the woman called Martha said reluctantly. 'I think he's finished eating.'

She stepped aside and pointed in the general direction of a back room. Brock went through to see a thin-faced man sitting at a table, an empty plate in front of him.

'I need your help, Doc,' he said without preamble. 'I got a friend who's hurt pretty bad. He needs patching up.'

Doc McLaine looked his visitor up and down.

'Where is he, this friend? If he's outside, bring him in.'

'No, he ain't outside, Doc. He's in no state to ride. We gotta hurry, he's in a bad way.'

Late night visits from strangers meant only one thing in Doc McLaine's book: there had been a shooting somewhere. He had done this sort of thing before and it would cost this stranger to patch up his friend. 'I'll get my bag.' He turned to his wife.

'I'll try to be home soon, Martha.'

McLaine followed his visitor out into the darkness and was surprised to see that there was already a horse waiting for him. He suddenly felt a pang of concern at the sight of a second rider. Why had his visitor not come alone? Did he think that the good doctor would need to be persuaded? If so, why?

'Come on, we gotta move!' snapped the second man, a mean-faced figure, McLaine thought. He was beginning to think that this wasn't such a good idea – whatever they were willing to pay.

'Where are we going?' he asked, reluctantly mounting the third horse.

'The Double D,' said Brock.

'Duggan's spread? And who's your injured friend? Not Joe Duggan himself, I hope.'

'Look, Doc, we ain't got time to sit here jawin'. Let's ride.'

The younger man rapped the rump of McLaine's horse and they headed out of town. Nobody who saw them go took any notice.

Doc McLaine had only once before visited the Double D and that had been to patch up the ill-tempered rancher who had been badly beaten in a bar-room brawl. He was lucky to be alive and probably would not have lasted the night if his foreman had not ridden into town and, just like now, taken him out to the ranch.

This time, though, he knew neither of the two men who had called on him at home; he did not know who the wounded man was, and he had a nervous feeling about the whole affair. But, like the others, he rode through the darkness in silence. They reached the outer fence of the Double D in bright moonlight and they were heading for the house when the bigger man spoke for the first time since leaving town.

He reached out and grabbed the reins of the doc's horse and forced it to a halt. 'Not to the house, Doc. This way.'

He pulled the horse off the main trail and led him into the bushes. McLaine felt fear rising. This had been a bad idea, but there was no backing away now. He would just do what he had to do, collect his money and leave. This was none of his business.

They travelled slowly along a narrow track for several minutes before coming to a clearing and a small shack. The big man dismounted and ordered the doc off his horse.

'He's in there,' Brock said, pointing towards the small cabin. 'Go fix him up.'

What awaited McLaine was a young man lying on a low bed in the corner of a small, dimly lit room. One quick look was enough to tell him that the kid was in a bad way. He was shaking with a high fever and after a quick examination McLaine knew that the wounded man needed urgent treatment. More than he could give.

He put down his bag and went outside. The two men who had called at his house were standing in the shadows smoking and talking in low tones.

'In here!' the doc called out. 'I'm going to need some help.'

The bigger man threw down his cheroot and hurried over.

McLaine reeled off his requirements – hot water, light, whiskey – and went back inside. The kid on the bed was muttering incoherently.

'When did this happen?' the doc asked.

'A day ago – maybe two,' said Sam Brock.

'Which was it?' McLaine said. 'You must remember. Where did it happen?'

Brock tried to control his rising anger.

'Look, Doc, this isn't your affair. Just patch the kid up and we'll be on our way.'

McLaine emitted a sharp scoffing sound.

'This man's going nowhere. Even if I get him patched up he'll be in no fit state to ride anywhere for at least a week. Now, let's get to it.'

The doc worked on the injured man, gingerly removing the bullet that had lodged close to his heart with a careful, delicate touch. The minutes dragged by and McLaine sweated profusely as he worked on the wound. But, by the time he had finished, almost an hour after his work started – he was satisfied that he had done all he could.

'All we can do now is pray,' he said, washing his hands clean of the injured man's blood, 'though I don't suppose that is part of your thinking.'

The big man ignored the jibe but said, 'When can we move him out of here?'

McLaine felt in control again; doctoring was his territory and even some of the hardest men realized that the doctor knew best when it came to mending wounds.

'If you want to kill him you can move him right now; if you want him to live then keep him here and warm for the next two or three days. I'll call back to see how he's progressing.'

Brock remained silent and thoughtful.

Complete with sheriff and posse. I can't let that happen.

'We'll make sure he's fine,' he said at last. He would move the kid to the big house. Duggan still owed him for his silence and offering them the use of a run-down shack came nowhere near to repaying that debt. He needed more.

Duggan's woman, who washed and cooked for him, among her other duties no doubt, would have to nurse the kid and although Duggan, reformed character though he claimed to be, might object, there was no other choice. If the doc was right the kid needed help and more rest. What concerned

64

Brock was the inevitable fate of the doctor. He had never thought of himself as a cold-blooded killer and felt there was some grain of honour in giving a man he was about to kill at least a chance to defend himself.

But Jess was different. He was a cold killer who would have butchered the rest of the stage passengers if Brock hadn't stopped him. Now Brock would need to use that heartless streak. He could not allow the doctor to report his night's work to the local law. It would not take long for the sheriff to connect it with the stage robbery and then all hell would break loose. The doctor would have to be silenced and that was a job for Jess.

'You've done a good job, Doc. The silly fool got into a fight with somebody who was quicker than him. Perhaps he'll learn to walk away after this.'

'I doubt it,' said McLaine, in an attempt to go along with the conversation. 'These kids never learn until it's too late.'

'Mebbe so,' Brock conceded as the doc finished packing away his instruments. 'You'll have a hard time finding your way back to town in the dark. 'I'll get my man to show you the way. Leave the horse at the livery.'

'There's no need,' McLaine protested. 'I'm sure I can find my own way.'

But the big man was insistent. 'It's no trouble.

Not after what you've done for the kid.'

Before he could protest further, Brock had left the shack. Waiting only a few seconds, McLaine then eased the door open.

He watched and strained his ears to listen as the two men spoke in hushed tones at the far corner of the small clearing. He couldn't hear what was being said but suspicions were growing that he was in danger. These men were on the run – of that he was certain – and that would make them desperate. But were they desperate enough to kill him? The fact that they were making no attempt to keep him prisoner, to have him come back to watch the wounded man's progress, strengthened the feeling that they meant to do him harm. Permanent harm. The offer of help to find his way back to town didn't fool him. Once out there in the darkness he would be in even greater danger.

Quietly, he slipped the door back off its latch. Behind him the man on the bed groaned, but he had no time to waste on him now. He had to get away.

He had no idea where the back door led but he would have to take his chance under the cover of darkness. If his luck held he could make good his escape before they had chance to track him down. If not . . . he could not bear to think about that.

McLaine checked that the two men were still

deep in conversation in the clearing at the front of the shack before creeping out on the other side. Once outside, McLaine hurried towards the thick undergrowth, but had made only a few yards when he heard the shout of alarm from behind. Brock had clearly gone back into the cabin and found the doc missing.

Fear gripped the medical man as he stumbled deeper into the bushes. Ahead was a wide clearing and, much to his consternation, the moon was high in the clear sky. No clouds to offer any cover. Crouching, he tried to edge his way into the open expanse, listening for any sound of his pursuers. He waited.

The minutes passed without any signs that he was being followed and McLaine felt himself breathing more easily. Satisfied that he was alone, he resumed his crouching scramble to safety. Another cluster of bushes brought him the security of darkness but he knew he couldn't stay there. They would find him and that meant only one thing: a bullet.

As his eyes became adjusted to the darkness, Doc McLaine tried to take in his surroundings. Ahead was a barren stretch of rocks, rising to a plateau. Beyond that he didn't know, but if he could clamber up the steep slope of the hill and down the other side he would surely be halfway to safety.

But even before he could make his first move

from the cover of the bushes, his heart missed a beat. Close by, a whispered voice came, 'He can't get far, Sam. We'll get him.'

McLaine froze. Fear gripped him again. The hunters were only a few feet away. Fear was followed almost immediately by panic. McLaine ditched his bag, rose from his position and, with one quick glance around, made a rush for safety. With each step, his confidence grew, his heart pounded and he saw in the moonlight the sanctuary of the rocks ahead. Closer . . . closer.

Breathlessly he forced his thin, aching body forward. He wanted to scream, to beg for mercy, to plead for his life. But by now he knew that would be useless. They would not let him walk free to tell the law that they had a wounded friend hiding in a cabin on the Double D ranch. Then it came . . . in the stillness of the night it sounded like thunder. But for the good doctor it meant the end. The first bullet hit him high on the right shoulder, ripping through bone and muscle.

He screamed.

The second caught him in the middle of the back. He was sent crashing, hitting the ground face first. Death brought a sudden end to all the pain.

Jess, sneering in ugly triumph, returned his Colt to its holster. Beside him, Sam Brock barked an order.

'Get him hidden. And make it good.'

He walked away, turning back towards the cabin. He always felt bad about violent death. The doc had done them no harm, but now he was dead. Jess would hide the body so deep in the undergrowth that he would not be found for days, if ever. By then he and his fellow stage robbers would be three states away. Guilt played no part in Sam Brock's philosophy. It was time to move on and that might mean he and Jess would be going their separate ways.

Slowly he trudged back to the cabin to check on the kid.

CHAPTER FIVE

Sheriff Naylor stirred at the sound of banging on his office door. He had slept badly during the night after the day's fruitless search for the stage robbers. He felt that US Marshal Wade had given up too easily, that he had other things on his mind.

Now, as he tried to catch a few minutes' rest in one of the empty cells at the back of the office, he was disturbed by urgent hammering, first on the door and then on the window. He struggled to his feet and made his way through the office. He was surprised to see his visitor was Martha McLaine. And she was in a state of panic.

Naylor had been sheriff of Virtue for more years than he could remember but he had never seen the doctor's wife in such an agitated state. She had always been known as Stonefaced Schoolma'am by the children she taught and by their parents. Emotion had never been any part of her make-up.

He ushered her into the office and pulled out a chair and helped her to sit.

Seeing her like this, even the hard-headed lawman felt a touch of anxiety.

'What is it, Martha? What's wrong?'

She sat silently for a moment and then, close to tears, she blurted out her fears.

'It's Cooper, Sheriff. He's ... he's missing. I mean, oh—' She started to sob before making a determined effort to pull herself together. She knew she had a reputation for being a cold-hearted woman and almost half the population wondered why Cooper McLaine hadn't packed his bags and hightailed it out of town years ago. But she knew differently, and his disappearance had nothing to do with the state of their long marriage.

'We had just finished our meal last night,' she began, making a supreme effort to keep her voice steady, 'when we had a visitor. I had never seen him before, a big man in a black shirt. He wanted Coop to go with him. Seems he had a friend who needed some help. Coop said he'd be home soon, but he hasn't come back. He's been gone all night and I don't know what to do.'

A man staying out all night was hardly an unusual event in Virtue but the sheriff knew that such a thought would never have crossed Cooper McLaine's mind. He wouldn't have dared.

'Steady, Martha. Try to keep calm. Did you get to hear where they were headed?'

'Nobody said. All I know is they rode out of town going west. There were two of them; the man who came into the house and the one who stayed outside with the spare horse to take Coop where they were going. They didn't even wait for him to get out the buckboard. I don't know what to do, Sheriff.'

Naylor continued to quiz the woman, but he soon saw that there was nothing she could say that would help find her missing husband. But experience told him one thing: that the doc had not been out all night of his own accord.

Naylor had much to occupy his thoughts as he led Martha McLaine out of the office with a sympathetic promise that he would do everything to find her husband, but that she should go straight home and inform him if Coop returned in the meantime. For a doctor to be called out of his home by a stranger late at night meant only one thing: a shooting. Somebody had taken a bullet and that immediately turned Naylor's mind back to the stage hold-up. It didn't take much imagination to come up with the opinion that suggested to Naylor that the robbers were still around. And although he had told Martha McLaine to go home and try to calm herself, he could not stop himself thinking the worst.

If the man who had called at the McLaine house the previous night had been one of the trio, the chances were that the doc was now just another of his victims. Naylor cursed aloud. If the doc had carried out his patching-up work successfully the chances are that they would be long gone by now.

The sheriff picked up his gunbelt and headed for the Kember Hotel. Wade may have been eager to abandon the search yesterday, but things were a lot different this morning.

Martha had said that the men had taken her husband west out of town and there were only two likely hiding spaces for fugitives in that direction.

There was the Big K of Hal Kember and the Duggan spread and there were dozens of possible hide-outs on both ranches but the latest information at least gave him a start.

Like Naylor, Adam Wade had a sleepless night but for a very different reason. For the second night he had shared a bed with the alluring Laura Kember. This woman was getting to him and he was sure that wasn't what he wanted. Kember's wife, no matter how appealing, was not part of his plans.

He had sensed that the sheriff was aggrieved by his suggestion to abandon the search but he felt that to continue would prove fruitless. Armed thieves, whether they robbed banks, trains or stages, did not stay in the vicinity of their crime longer than necessary and almost two days had passed since the hold-up.

After returning his horse to the livery on the edge of town Adam strolled back to the Kember. He was just about to enter the hotel when three riders, clearly in a hurry, galloped past and headed out of town. He paid no heed.

Inside, the main room was almost deserted. Two locals were standing at the long bar and only one of the card tables was occupied. There was no sign of Luke Kember.

Adam stopped for a beer and was involved in a friendly conversation with the bartender when she came down the staircase. Heads turned – as he suspected they always did when Laura entered a room. She smiled at the sight of him and he raised his glass in ackowledgement. Again he was impressed with the auburn-haired woman in the sleek off-shoulder dress. He suddenly became aware of his own dust-covered, unshaven appearance.

She didn't seem to notice as she nodded pleasantly to her other customers before joining him at the end of the bar. They both ignored the knowing looks of the few drinkers in the room as they settled at one of the empty tables.

They had been talking about nothing in particular until Adam suddenly said, 'For the wife of a rich rancher you don't spend much time at home, Laura.'

She looked at him squarely. 'You don't need to know why. Hal and I have an agreement. He lets me run this place and I let him get on with his ranch and his politicking. What else is there to know?'

'Just that if I had a woman like you I would want her by my side – not running some saloon.'

She smiled. 'Hotel,' she corrected him, 'and you haven't met Hal, have you? He's fine with the way things are.'

Adam didn't believe that. No man with a wife like Laura would sit back and allow her to run loose in a town of cattlemen and drifters.

Or even deputy US marshals.

Then there was Luke. Why was she so sure that he wouldn't eventually report back to his father, even if it was only out of spite?

Her stepson was not the sort of man to be trusted. And how long could Adam stop himself from telling her that the real reason for his visit to Virtue was to avenge the death of his father by killing Hal Kember?

As he followed her up the staircase he wondered if he might not need to tell her. . . .

They spent long hours of the night enjoying each other before eventually falling asleep. Now, while he studied her naked body as she bathed in her private room, Adam decided that what she didn't know wouldn't harm her. When the deed was done he would be on his way out of her life for good. She would move on and, from what he had learned so far, she wouldn't spend too many hours mourning her husband.

He was eating his usual steak and eggs breakfast in the back room of the hotel when the sheriff hurried into the room and outlined the details behind the previous night's disappearance of Doctor McLaine.

Naylor's opinion made sense to Adam. Nobody called on a doctor at night unless there was an emergency and, in Adam's experience, that usually meant a shooting. There had been gun play at the stage hold-up and one of the robbers had been wounded. It was likely that he would need attention so the chances were that his fellow raiders had called on the nearest doctor: Cooper McLaine was the only medical man within a day's ride.

As the two lawmen rode out of town on the same trail taken by the night riders, Naylor explained, 'I didn't say it to Martha, but I don't expect to find Coop alive. Once he's done his job they won't be wanting him to tell the world where they are hiding out.'

Adam agreed. Killers didn't take chances so the doc's hopes of surviving were pretty low.

It was then that Sheriff Naylor gave Adam the

news he wasn't expecting.

'Our first call will be the Big K and Hal Kember.'

The showdown with the man who had murdered his father six years earlier was now less than an hour's ride away. It was now that Adam questioned his own commitment to the cause of vengeance. Only time would tell.

The ride to the Big K was made in silence until Naylor, as if tipped by the thoughts going through Adam's head, said, 'I still don't know why you're in Virtue, Marshal. Maybe it's time you let me know.'

And maybe it isn't, Adam thought, so instead he told the local lawman what he wanted him to believe . . . that he was on the trail of a wanted rustler after a tip that the man had been seen in the territory.

Naylor was puzzled. He knew the name and crimes of every wanted man who had ever passed through Virtue and he didn't know of any wanted cattle rustler. And if that was the God's honest truth, why keep it a secret? But he let it pass.

The entrance to the Kember ranch was decorated by a huge HK branding iron and was patrolled by a rifle-carrying cowhand.

'Ike Blake, ain't it?' said the sheriff, as the two riders pulled their horses to a stop. 'We're here to see Hal.'

The man with the Winchester looked first at the sheriff and then at his companion.

'He's up at the big house, Sheriff, but you may be out of luck. He's got company. Lots of it. All those ranchers and campaign fellers who are backing him for the Congress are up there. Which is why I'm here – make sure nobody gets through who ain't invited.'

'We ain't invited, Ike, but we're going in just the same. I'll explain to Hal.'

The ranch hand lowered his rifle, pulled back the gate and let the two lawmen through.

As they approached the main house it became clear that Ike Blake hadn't been exaggerating. The drive in front of the veranda along the white, neat, low-slung building was crowded with buckboards, tied up horses and carriages.

Hal Kember did indeed have a lot of visitors to support him in his attempt to become a congress-man.

They dismounted and climbed the steps leading into the house. Raised voices came from inside the building. Apparently all was not going to plan.

'You can't do that, Hal!' somebody shouted. 'It ain't gonna work.'

A smooth, even-toned voice came clearly in answer. 'Calm down, Bart. It's only an idea to get the others on our side. Once we're in, well . . .

promises are made to be broken.'

The chuckles that followed confirmed that the others agreed that they had a politician in their midst; a man who would look after their interests in the capital.

Naylor removed his hat as they entered the large splendidly furnished room. The chuckling stopped and all heads turned towards the new arrivals. Slowly, the men standing around the large table moved aside to reveal the owner of the Big K. He was seated in an invalid chair and was much older that Adam had expected. He wore his grey hair long and his moustache was untidy. He was a lot heavier than the man Adam remembered from that fateful night in Crawford Gap. And unlike the cruel, stone-faced figure on that night, he was smiling.

'Sheriff Naylor. Come in, bring your friend—'

'Wade,' said Naylor, 'US deputy marshal.'

Adam hoped to detect some recognition at the mention of his name but there was none.

'And what can we do for you, Sheriff? It's a day for being helpful, as my friends here will tell you.' Almost everybody in the company laughed. Naylor shuffled from foot to foot, acting as though he was in the presence of greatness. Adam had no such inhibitions.

He was staring into the eyes of the man who had killed his father. And wheelchair or not, it took all his self-control to keep his six-gun holstered. He felt the anger, the thirst for revenge, growing inside him but he knew that this was not the right time with Kember surrounded by thirty or more of his close supporters.

It was Naylor who broke the rising tension inside Adam.

'We need your help, Hal, the deputy marshal and me. You may have heard about the raid on the stage a couple of days back. They gunned down the driver and a passenger and we think the killers are still around. Last night somebody called on the doc and he's still missing.'

'And you reckon I might know something that can help, Sheriff?'

Naylor grinned. 'Not exactly, Hal. But from what we know three men rode west out of town late last night. This is the first possible hiding place. One of your old barns or such.

'We would like you to let us have a good look-see. We ain't got much to go on, but—'

Hal Kember held up his hand.

'You know me, Jack, anything I can do to help the law,' he interrupted. 'Do you need any of my men?'

Naylor looked at Adam. 'We could do with some help.'

'Thanks, Mr Kember, but we'll be fine. If you could just point us in the direction of any likely hide-outs . . . old deserted shacks, that sort of thing.'

Hal Kember thought for a moment then slapped the arms of his chair.

'As you can see, Marshal, I don't get round too much these days, but if you see my son, he'll give you the details you need.'

'Your son? Would that be Luke?'

Kember looked surprised. 'You know Luke?'

'We've met,' said Adam coolly.

Hal Kember chuckled. 'And I can see you weren't too impressed. Luke's a bit of a wild thing, but no more than we were at his age. You'll find him out back, doing his useless best to break a bronco; more likely to break his fool neck, but I can't stop him. Now, if you two gents will excuse me, I have business to attend to with my other visitors.'

Once outside, Adam considered what he had discovered. His father's killer was confined to a wheelchair; he had all the appearances of a tower of the community; he was more than willing to assist in tracking down the stage robbers, even offering his son's help, though Adam wasn't so sure that was going to make finding the fugitives any easier.

A regular pillar of society, the sort of cattleman who would make a perfect congressman. Except for that snippet of conversation they had overheard on the way into the house.

Promises are made to be broken: that had been

the voice of Hal Kember.

Luke was not hard to find. The shouting and whistling from an area at the back of the house led the two men to a corral. A group of cowhands were sitting on a fence urging on a young cowboy who was inside the pen trying to bring a stubborn bronco under control. That young cowboy was Luke Kember. It was a one-sided battle and the horse was having by far the best of things.

Adam and Naylor joined the cheering spectators who were clearly enjoying seeing their boss's son being given the runaround. Adam could see why. Young Kember was hopelessly out of his depth as he tried to bring the horse under control. Three times he was sent tumbling into the dust before finally losing his self control. Screaming and cursing, he reached for a whip and starting lashing out at the startled animal. The cheering and the whistling stopped; the onlookers fell silent and the only voice was that of a screeching Luke Kember. Nobody moved as the frightened horse panicked and reared up. Luke was in an uncontrollable rage as he lifted the whip back over his shoulder. It went no further as Adam leapt over the fence and grabbed the thongs, wrenching the whip from the younger man's grasp.

Startled, Luke turned to face his assailant. There was hate in his eyes. 'You! Are you crazy? That horse is wild. I'm breaking it!'

'Not like that, you ain't, sonny,' said Adam quietly. 'You'll be lucky if it doesn't kick you to death.' Angrily, he threw the whip aside.

In the far corner of the corral the horse stood snorting angrily and staring, wild eyed, as the two men faced each other.

'What's it to do with you, mister? You're on my land.'

Adam smiled. 'Your land? I thought this was Hal Kember's ranch.'

'What's his is mine. He'll have you horse-whipped.'

Adam thought about that before saying, 'Yeah, I really think he would. But he isn't here right now, young Luke, so I suggest you get going before I change my mind and let that bronc loose on you – without the whip.'

Luke was trying to keep his temper under control. He knew that the men were watching his every move, wondering how he would take care of this interfering stranger.

'I'm warning you – you ain't heard the last of this. Once I tell the old man what I know about you and that cheating bitch of a wife of his—'

Suddenly, Adam allowed his temper to get out of control. He reached forward, grabbed Luke's shirt front and dragged him so that their faces were only an inch apart.

'Before you do that, just remember, I think I might still owe you a bullet,' he snapped in the other's face.

Then he pushed Luke away and the younger man fell backwards into the dust. Luke scrambled to his feet, his control now completely lost as he lunged at Adam. But the bigger man coolly and swiftly side-stepped, pushed his hand into the other's neck and sent him sprawling, this time face down into the dirt.

All around, the ranch hands turned away silently. They knew better than to join in the humiliation of the owner's son. Briefly Adam stood contemptu-ously over the sprawled Luke then turned his back, climbed the fence and rejoined the sheriff who had watched the action in silence.

'Looks like we'll have to find our own way around the spread, without Luke's help,' Naylor grinned. 'I guess you don't like the kid, huh?'

Adam returned the grin. 'You could say that. And judging from the looks I'm getting the feeling is mutual.'

They turned to see Luke dusting himself down and if looks could kill Adam would have fallen dead on the spot. Instead, the two lawmen returned to their horses and set about the search for the missing doctor – and whoever he had tended to the previ-ous night.

*

Less than an hour's ride away, Sam Brock and Joe Duggan sat on the veranda of the Double D ranch house and talked of the war. Both men had spent the best part of four years fighting for the Confederate cause and both had come through it unscathed.

They had been with Quantrill's Raiders at the Lawrence Massacre in '63 when they had crossed the Missouri-Kansas border and butchered nearly 300 local citizens. When Quantrill was eventually killed in Kentucky, the pair went their separate ways, Brock linking up with the James Gang while Duggan joined a cattle drive heading west.

It was three years later when the two men crossed paths again. Brock was still a fugitive from the law and the Union authorities had put a price on his head.

By this time, Duggan was a trail boss, respected by his men and cattle owners alike. But still a man with a shady past. It was that shady past that had led Brock to keep a close watch on his activities, even after he became the owner of the Double D.

Duggan poured them each another whiskey. He was uncomfortable. He hoped he had seen the last of Brock, but for more than ten years he had made regular visits – each time bringing more bad news.

This time it was a wounded kid, shot in the chest in a stage robbery only a few miles away on the road to Virtue.

He hadn't banked on this when he had told Brock what he had managed to overhear on his last visit into the town's bank: that the stage would be bringing in the railmen's monthly payroll. Sure, Brock had promised him a cut, but he hadn't wanted it – he just wanted Brock and his like out of his hair once and for all. He had been a fool: he must have known that was not how things worked in Brock's world.

Now, just like every other time, Brock reminded Duggan that their shared secret was safe as long as he co-operated. Joe Duggan knew he had no choice.

'We should be on our way in a coupla days,' Brock reminded him. 'Soon as the kid is fit to ride, we'll be outa your hair, Joe.'

But for how long, Duggan thought? Until the next time there's trouble, then Sam would come calling? Just like he always did. Also, he didn't like the look of Brock's latest sidekick, Jess. Too trigger-happy, he guessed. He spent his time perched on the corral fence, fingering his long-barrelled Colt and practising his speed of draw. Duggan expected him to be dead before he reached the age of twenty-five.

'Katy'll take good care of him, Sam, but he may need the doc again. He doesn't seem to have got much better since you brought him in.'

Sam had not mentioned that the doctor was buried somewhere in the shrub on the fringe of the Double D, gunned down by the young man out there on the corral fence.

'Tell me, Sam, who did the shooting at the stage hold-up? I'm guessing it wasn't you. Was it the kid inside?'

Brock emptied his glass and poured himself another drink. 'Best you don't know, Joe. 'Sides, it don't matter much. If they catch us we all hang.'

'In that case, the sooner your injured friend is fit enough to ride, the better.' Duggan finished his drink. Having stage robbers and killers around reminded him too much of his past. He thought he'd left all this behind.

It was then that the gun-happy Jess leapt down from the fence and ran towards the two men on the veranda.

'Sam! Joe! Riders coming!'

The search of the outbuildings of the Big K turned out to be fruitless for Adam and the sheriff. The run-in with Luke Kember had forced them to carry on without any help and it had taken longer than they had expected to end up finding nothing.

'We'll try again tomorrow,' Adam suggested. He had given a lot of thought to his next move. His run-in with Luke had only added strength to his resolve to make the Kember family pay for the death of his father. The years since the murder in Crawford Gap should have eased the pain for Adam but the anger had grown in him ever since he came face to face with the man who had carried it out. Hal Kember might be confined to a wheel-chair, but that did not make him any less guilty: the time was not far away when he would have to confront the old man.

His thoughts were interrupted by the sheriff.

'There's still some daylight. We keep looking.'

Adam could find no reason to argue. He was only here to help and this was the sheriff's call. He had found his own quarry and Hal Kember was going nowhere. That was his only interest now.

They rode on, checked two more rundown shacks without any result. The sheriff dismounted close to a brook and studied the landscape while his horse enjoyed a well-earned drink.

'The Double D is out that way,' he said, pointing towards a steep rise in the direction of the setting sun. 'Maybe we can give them a call. You never know, Joe Duggan may have seen something.' It was as though he was merely thinking aloud but Adam took up the idea.

'Let's pay him a visit,' he said, digging his heels into his horse.

Duggan rose from his seat and walked down the steps of his veranda to meet his visitors. Brock and his snarling sidekick Jess had acted swiftly at the first sight of the two riders; their horses were now hidden in a barn while they joined their wounded friend in a room at the back of the house.

The two men dismounted and left their steeds to enjoy another much needed rest and a drink at a trough.

'Evenin', Sheriff. What brings you way out here?' Duggan was politeness itself as he shook hands with the Virtue lawman.

Naylor introduced Adam. Strangely, Adam had a vague idea that he had seen this man before but he dismissed the thought almost immediately. He had far more important things on his mind. 'We're looking for Doc McLaine, Joe. Don't suppose he's passed this way, mebbe – last night.'

'The doc? No, I ain't called him out. You mean he's gone missing?'

'S'right. He went out with a couple of strangers and he hasn't been seen since.'

'What makes you think he'd be out this way? Like I said, I haven't called him out here.'

'Oh, no real reason. We just know they all headed

west out of town and after Kember's place, yours is the next spot on the trail.'

'Sorry, Sheriff, but, like I said, I haven't seen him.'

Adam spoke for the first time.

'And you haven't seen any strangers riding by? One of them carrying a bullet in his chest.'

'Nope. Don't get many strangers this far out. What's this about, Sheriff?'

'There's been a stage hold-up, Joe. Driver and a passenger were gunned down. One of the raiders was shot up and we don't think he can have got far without being patched up.'

'Sorry I can't help, Jack. I could ask my men out on the range to keep their eyes open and report in if they see anybody.'

Adam spoke again.

'Now we've come this far, you wouldn't mind if we took a look around?'

The suggestion took Duggan by surprise but he didn't show it. Instead, he said confidently, 'Sure, you can take a look but you won't find anybody skulking around here. I think I'd have noticed three riders, one of them carrying a bullet.'

'Suppose so,' Adam conceded. 'Well, Sheriff, it's getting late. We oughta get back to town. You never know, old Doc McLaine may have turned up safe and sound by now and we'd be wasting our time.'

The three men nodded and Duggan stood on his veranda and watched as the two lawmen rode away.

They were well out of earshot before Adam said, 'He's lying, Sheriff. Duggan knows something and I think you're goin' to have to deputize a few towns-folk to form that posse we talked about.' Naylor said nothing but waited for Adam to go on.

'How else would he know we're looking for three stage robbers? Neither of us told him.'

'So you reckon that they've passed this way?' asked Naylor.

'Either that, or they're still here and hiding in the house.'

Duggan waited for the two visitors to disappear from view before turning and hurrying into the house.

His woman, Katy, was tending to the injured man, feeding him soup, while Brock and Jess were play-ing cards.

'They gone?' asked Brock, looking up as Duggan came into the room.

'We need to talk, Sam.' He looked at Jess and Katy and then added, 'Alone.'

'Hold it!' Jess was on his feet in an instant. 'You ain't leavin' me out.'

A cold look from Brock silenced Jess and he slumped back into his seat. As the older men left the room, Brock could guess what was coming. Duggan tried to keep calm. He knew that losing his temper would only antagonize Brock and that was the last thing he needed.

Having three fugitives on his ranch was bad enough – but one of them knew enough about him to cause him big trouble. And he didn't need trouble.

'You didn't tell me about the doc,' Duggan said, as the two men stepped out into the deepening darkness. 'What's happened to him?'

Brock shrugged. 'That was unlucky; Jess just got carried away. But don't worry, they won't find him.'

'Which means they'll be back, Sam. You gotta get out of here. Tonight.'

'The kid ain't fit to ride anywhere,' Brock protested.

'Leave the kid. Katy'll take care of him. Look, Sam, I don't need any shooting out here. I'm settled here, a peace-loving citizen.'

Brock chuckled. 'Not like the old days, then, when you an' me rode together. Lucky for you I've kept quiet about those days, Joe.'

Duggan sighed. He knew that was coming but he was ready. 'That won't do either of us any good if they come back with a posse.'

Brock thought for a moment. It was true he could be well away from the Double D by daybreak and

leave the kid to the mercy of a posse or lynch mob.
But, despite his life on the wrong side of the law, he
still had some scruples. Unlike Jess, he knew about
loyalty and he felt he owed the kid something. Even
so . . . he was tempted.

Was Joe Duggan trying to scare him off with talk
of a posse? He listened in silence while the rancher
continued his effort to persuade his old friend that
it was no longer safe to stay around.

He knew that if he put the idea to Jess he would
be all for getting out, picking up the strongbox
from its hiding place in the hills, splitting the cash
two ways and heading out of the state.

'I guess this means you won't be wanting your
share,' Brock suggested, as the pair returned to the
back room where Jess was sulking at being left out
of he conversation. Duggan said nothing and Brock
went over to where Katy was feeding the kid.

'How's he coming along?'

Katy, a pleasant-faced matronly woman who,
Brock suspected, had no idea of Duggan's past,
tried to look on the bright side.

'Maybe he can move in a day or two. He's still
very weak though; he needs building up if you men
have a long journey in front of you.' The kid tried
to sit upright but fell back at the first attempt.

'I'll be fine soon, Sam. We can be on our way
when you say.'

'Easy, son. We're going nowhere till you're ready to ride.'

Jess stepped in. 'You heard him, Sam. He's ready. We can saddle up and be out of here tonight.'

Brock gripped the gunman's arm, squeezing his bicep. He was beginning to regret having Jess along. It had been fine at first. Like the kid who was now nursing a chest wound, he had been keen to learn, to take advice. Now he thought he knew it all and he was becoming a liability. 'We go when I say,' Brock said, in an effort to keep the anger out of his voice. 'We'll talk about it tomorrow.' He turned towards the bed. 'Meantime, kid you try to get some sleep.'

Jess skulked out of the room, leaving Brock to nursemaid the kid. His patience was growing thin and if Sam didn't move out in the next day he would go his own way. He knew where they had stashed the strongbox. He didn't need Sam or the kid. The idea began to grow in Jess's mind as he went out on to the veranda to light a cheroot. For too long he had relied on Sam for everything he did; every bank raid or train robbery had been his idea, his organization. Well, no more. After this, he would go it alone.

He was a big boy now. To hell with Sam. And to hell with the kid. Jess threw his half-finished smoke into the dust and headed for the barn. It would soon be time for action.

Adam and Naylor arrived back in Virtue after night-fall and the town was quiet at the end of another hot and sultry day. Adam left his horse at the livery with instructions to have it fed and groomed. He was making his way back to his room at the hotel – and maybe another night in the company of Laura – when he was distracted by a moving shape in the shadows.

He stopped in his tracks and after standing still for a few moments he thought he might have imag-ined it. Even so he took the precaution of stepping off the raised boardwalk and into the middle of main street. He increased his stride.

He was passing the saloon, now in semi darkness when ... there it was again. A figure dodging between the buildings.

His hand went down to feel the assurance of his holstered sixgun. The hotel was within a few of his lengthened strides, but he didn't quite make it. Suddenly, from over his left shoulder he heard the pounding of rushing feet. He spun round – there were three of them – all big, all masked, and all armed with wooden stakes.

Adam crouched, bracing himself. He swerved and ducked cleverly to avoid the first wildly swing-ing attacker, but the second caught him on his left shoulder sending a stabbing pain through his body. His fist closed around the butt of his gun but the third masked man, lashing out, smashed the stake across his right arm. Adam dropped to one knee as the blows rained down on him.

But somehow he managed to grapple a stake away from one of his assailants. He swung hopefully and sent one of the men staggering backwards, cursing. Another crushing blow to the side of the face sent Adam into the dirt, blood oozing from the wound in his cheek. He tried to get to his feet but a swinging boot caught him in the ribs, knocking the breath out of his body.

One of the men rammed a fist into his face, smashing his nose. More blood. More pain. Instinct told him that he was now in a fight for his life, but how would it end? When they had beaten him to a pulp? Or when they had killed him? Desperately he lashed out in blind hope of connecting with muscle or bone.

Using the stick he had snatched away from one of the attackers, he managed to hit a target, but another kick to his stomach had him doubled up in pain. He lay there blindly helpless, his eyes swollen closed, when suddenly he was aware that the three attackers had been joined by a fourth man.

'Leave him!' the newcomer snarled. 'He's mine now.'

Adam was aware that the trio were backing off, but before he could move, the attack started again. This time he was being whipped. Then kicked.

The fourth man swung a boot into his groin and followed this with another whip lashing.

'Bastard! Now who's the big man? Now let's see how good you are at bedding that bitch!' Another crack of the whip; a vicious array of spittle and another boot to the stomach sent Adam into oblivion. But not before he recognized the voice of the fourth man who had let others do his dirty work before stepping in to finish off the evil attack. And there were other voices – a woman screaming, men yelling, the sound of footsteps dashing towards the disturbance.

If he got through this, Adam knew he would look forward to the day when he made Luke Kember pay. It was then he passed out.

CHAPTER SIX

Slowly, reluctantly, Adam opened his eyes. The pain was excruciating. His ribs ached and the kick in the groin had sickened him. His back and shoulders, brutally beaten by the stick-wielding thugs, ached almost beyond endurance. His vision was blurred but he could just make out the face of the woman leaning over him.

Laura Kember had heard the commotion in the street, but as she stepped out of the hotel she saw four men running into the darkness beyond the Diamond Saloon. A man, beaten to a pulp, was lying in the street. Had they left him for dead?

Hurrying out she leaned over the crumpled heap that was the man who had shared her bed these last two nights. Adam Wade made no sound as she knelt beside him.

Returning to the hotel, she summoned the help of her bartender and customers and together they carried the injured man to his room. Now, six hours later as dawn was breaking over the eastern ridge, there were the first signs of life from the stricken marshal.

She mopped his bruised and bloodied face with a cold cloth and pressed him firmly back as he tried to lift himself on to one elbow.

'Easy, Marshal,' she said soothingly. 'You wouldn't make it to the edge of the bed.'

He smiled and it hurt sickeningly.

'You must have really upset somebody.'

Adam fingered his bruised and swollen face and tried to move, but the pain grew worse. He closed his eyes again and flopped back on to the bed. The next thing he heard was the voice of Sheriff Naylor. He was talking to Laura.

'Nobody saw anything. The saloon was quiet and the street was empty. Whoever did this knew how to pick their time and place. They must have been waiting for him to leave his horse at the livery.'

Then Laura said, 'I saw four of them running off but it was too dark to make out anybody for sure. I heard them riding off: they must have had their horses tied up and waiting behind the Diamond.'

'Which way did they ride out?'

'West, I think,' she answered.

'Seems a popular way out of town,' said Naylor. 'First the two men who took off with our doc; now these four who gave our marshal here a good beating.'

Adam listened to all this but kept his eyes closed and said nothing. The road west led past the Kember place and that was all he needed to know.

Luke's sneers were still fresh in his mind.

'We'll leave him to rest; maybe he can tell us something when he's feeling better. Meantime, I have to get a posse together. The marshal had a feeling that our stage robbers were holed up at the Duggan place. Could be right, I reckon. Or they could be someplace else. Who knows?'

Adam kept his eyes closed and waited for the sound of the sheriff leaving and the door closing behind him. Eventually, he was alone with Laura.

He lifted himself up and grimaced with the pain that racked his entire body. She sat on the edge of the bed and again pressed her hand firmly on his chest.

'Lie still. Remember we don't have a doctor to patch you up. But if he was here he would tell you to take some rest.'

'But he's not here, Laura. Which mean you'll have to take his place. You'll have to stick me back together. Strap up my ribs. I have to get out of here. I've got some business to attend to and the sooner the better.'

'Don't be a fool, Adam. You can hardly walk let

alone ride a horse.'

Then, a thought suddenly struck her. 'You know who did this, don't you? You're going after them. Are you crazy? They'll kill you next time.'

'I know one of them,' Adam said quietly. 'That's enough.'

'Who was it? Who did this?'

Adam thought for a moment but then said, 'It's best you don't know.'

Reluctantly, Laura dressed Adam's wounds and strapped up his ribs. Gradually he was able to sit on the bed and breathe a lot easier. Within an hour he felt he was ready to visit the Big K ranch and confront Hal Kember and his rebellious son. And he did not mind which came first.

But although his breathing was slowly improving, Adam had to wonder if what he had planned was the result of his desire for instant revenge. The beating he had taken left him in no state to challenge Luke Kember to a physical contest. That way there was only more pain, or even worse. Facing him on his own turf – the Big K – was foolhardy at best and suicidal at worst.

And even if he survived his run-in with Luke and the ranch hands who had carried out the beating, there was the inevitable showdown with old man Kember to follow.

Adam had decided that he was not the man to

walk in and gun down another man whatever the provocation – though the haunting, harrowing experience of seeing his father dragged to his death was more than enough provocation. But Kember was confined to a wheelchair so even the satisfaction of standing face to face in a fair duel shoot-out was to be denied him.

Could he let it go at that? Could he simply ride off without letting Kember know that he was offering more than the rancher turned politician deserved . . . that he was offering to spare his life?

He also knew he could not ride away without giving young Luke the thrashing he deserved.

Eventually he allowed Laura to guide him gingerly back to the bed. 'Maybe you're right,' he said resignedly. 'Maybe I am crazy. What I have in mind can wait awhile.'

Naylor's hastily organized posse had no luck tracking the fugitives. Adam Wade's hunch that they were somewhere on the Double D failed to be backed up by any evidence, so Virtue's ageing lawman was left with no alternative but to abandon the search. He telegraphed the stage company's offer of a $3000 reward for information leading to the arrest of the robbers to all towns within a two-day ride of Virtue, but he expected that to be the last he would hear of the crime or the killers. Life in

Virtue would return to normal and his job would, as in the past, involve nothing more serious than the arrest and next day release of Saturday night drinkers and brawlers spilling out of the Diamond.

Like Adam Wade, fate had a different future mapped out for him than he imagined.

The following day, after a long rest and help of the soothing touch of Laura, Adam strode out of the Kember Hotel and headed for the livery where he collected his neatly groomed and well-rested horse and set off for the Big K on the journey that would settle his future.

CHAPTER SEVEN

Joe Duggan cursed the day he had allowed himself to become beholden to Sam Brock and was now paying a high price for his silence. He had always known that his old partner would be trouble and the passing of time had not changed the situation, Brock was still a threat and after the second visit of the sheriff – this time with his posse – he was more determined than ever to get the three men off his land the first chance he got.

The kid had recovered enough to ride out and the one they called Jess was anxious to be gone. There was nothing to keep them now, except . . . It was Brock who had raised the subject as they emerged from their hiding place to see the dust of the posse disappear over the ridge. 'That's the last we'll see of our friendly lawman. He won't be back again,' he said, as Duggan joined the three men.

'That leaves the trail clear. You could ride out

tonight,' the rancher suggested, but he did not get the response he had hoped for.

'There's no hurry, now, Joe. Like I said, he won't be coming back this way. Which means we can stay around for a few more days until they give up roaming the hills in the hope of running into us.'

Duggan tried another line.

'Trouble, Sam. My hands will be gettin' to thinkin' about you three. So far they've kept their noses outa my business. But I don't know how much longer that'll be the case.'

Brock rested his arm around the other man's shoulder. 'I'm sure you can handle that, Joe. After all, you know what it would mean if they found out about you and me.'

'Sure,' said Duggan quietly, well aware of the threat in Brock's voice. For years Duggan had stayed on the right side of the law, building up his ranch from nothing. Now, it was under threat from a man who had once been his friend. He walked away and headed back to the house. He had to think of a way of getting rid of the fugitives and sowing the seeds of possible capture in the mind of the one called Jess appeared to be the best hope of achieving that.

The chance came late in the afternoon when Jess walked away from the table after they had eaten the stew Katy had reluctantly prepared for her unwelcome visitors and made his way out to the corral.

Duggan lingered at the table just long enough to avoid any suspicion from the kid or Sam that he was following and made his way outside. Jess was leaning on the fence, smoking a cheroot and staring out at the landscape.

Duggan sidled up to him but immediately got the impression that his company wasn't welcome – which was a good thing; it meant that Jess was eager to get away.

'I think Sam's wrong, Jess,' the rancher said as an opening gambit. 'About the sheriff not coming back here. Once he's searched everywhere else and come up empty-handed he'll be back.'

Jess snarled his reply. 'Tell that to Sam. We've been here four days now and I want out, but he's gotten it into his head that we can stay here for as long as we want to. Says you're an old friend from way back and everything's fine. You saying it ain't?'

Duggan knew he had to be careful. He wanted this man on his side. 'No, I'm not saying that, Jess. Only I've been trying to tell Sam that my men are getting curious. Three strangers, a sheriff's posse and a stage hold-up . . . they ain't gonna stay quiet for much longer. And now there's the local doc who's gone missing.'

Jess flicked the remains of his cheroot into the dust.

'Maybe you're right. I've been wanting to move

on since we got here, but the kid—'

'The kid's fine now,' Duggan interrupted. 'He's fit to ride. Hell, he's been out there practising his gunplay.' Then, 'Maybe you should have another word with Sam. Your loot's just lying out there waiting to be picked up.'

Jess was thinking it over when Duggan added, 'And if they find the doc it won't be a posse that comes back – it'll be a lynch mob.'

For all his apparent bravado, Jess was no fool and the thought of being chased by a mob aiming to hang him was enough to persuade him that he would speak to Sam. He would convince him that it was time to move out. He could not be sure that they wouldn't find the doc's body.

True he had dumped the dead man deep in the bushes in a shallow grave, but it was close to the shack and any saddle tramp might stumble across it.

Duggan pushed harder. 'One thing, Jess: don't let Sam know it was my idea that you should hit the trail. He wouldn't take kindly to that.'

Jess grunted a token reply and the rancher watched him go as he headed for the house. As he stood there, his back to the corral fence, he tried to think over his next move if Sam insisted on staying put. That would end in gun play and bloodshed and he knew from experience that Sam Brock could handle himself in a shoot-out.

*

Adam's ride to the Big K was slow and at times painful. Twice he stopped along the trail to rest his aching limbs and took the time out to think about what was lying ahead of him. Gunning down Kember in cold blood had never been an option; taking him back to the little town of Crawford Gap to stand trial for a six-year-old murder was even less of a possibility. The most he could expect out of his mission to avenge his father's death was to let the killer know that he knew. And the least he could do by way of revenge was to destroy Kember's ambitions of becoming a congressman. Not much in return for a father's life cruelly and viciously cut short by a drunken cattleman on a rowdy night.

As for the son, Luke Kember . . . well, there was a score he *could* settle.

The pain of the beating he had received was a sharp, lingering reminder that the young Kember was heading down the track that led to a life outside the law. Not that he should let that worry him – the Kembers as a law-abiding family was not something that should concern him. Even the delectable Laura was a law unto herself.

An hour later he reached the impressive gates that led to the Kember spread. This time there was no armed guard to protect the would-be congressman from unwanted visitors and Adam rode slowly up to the big house without running into a single cowhand. The place appeared to be totally deserted as he dismounted and hitched his horse to a rail, looking around for signs of life but, apart from a couple of horses grazing lazily nearby, there was none.

Adam slowly climbed the steps and called out. No reply. Curious, he went inside the house. Even if all the hands were out fence-mending or rounding up strays he would have expected to find somebody in the main house.

He was about to give up and leave when he heard a sound from the back of the house. He called out again and this time there was an answer. A cry for help. Adam went through the house to a small yard at the back where he found the man he was looking for. Hal Kember was lying beside his upturned wheelchair.

Without a word, Adam walked swiftly down the steps, righted the chair and lifted Kember back into his seat.

'What happened?' Adam tried to sound concerned.

Kember eyed up his visitor before answering. 'Aren't you the marshal who came with Naylor the other day? You look as though you've been havin' a bad time ever since.'

Adam ignored the jibe. 'I'll survive. What happened to you?'

'Damn fool thing. I took this chair too near the edge and it toppled over.'

He wasn't going to tell this stranger the real reason he was sprawling in the dirt at the back of his house.

Left there by his drunken son after a squabble over gambling debts.

Luke had lost his temper, pushed him down the steps and left him lying there as he went off in search of more trouble.

'Anyways, thanks,' Kember said, regaining his breath. 'What you doing here, still looking for those stage robbers?'

Adam perched himself on the rail of the back yard veranda.

'Not this time . . . this time it's personal.'

Kember's puzzled look gave Adam a strange sense of superiority that he was going to enjoy.

'I guess this is about my son,' said the man in the chair. 'You better wheel me inside and we can have a drink and talk about it.'

Once inside, Adam said, 'Luke's only the half of it. I owe him for this.' He pointed to his bruised face. 'And some more.'

Kember made a snorting sound and said, 'Luke didn't do that all by himself, that's for sure. He ain't got the guts to take a grown man on face to face. But you said he's only half of it. What's the other?'

'You.'

Kember said nothing.

Adam went on, 'Remember a town called Crawford Gap?'

'Nope. Should I?'

'Probably not, but let me give your memory a push. My father was the sheriff of Crawford Gap on a night a group of drunken cowboys took over the place, smashing the saloon and wrecking stores. He went out to have a word with them, all reasonable and friendly like. He went out unarmed to tell them that they were welcome so long as they behaved.'

He paused for a reaction but there was none.

'They didn't do as they were asked and eventually, shooting and smashing wasn't enough for them. They came to the house and my father went out to see them again. He was unarmed and trying to be reasonable. But they weren't ready to listen to some small town tin star. For his trouble he was roped and dragged through the street by a man in a long black coat while the cattle drivers cheered. The rider eventually released him at the front door of his own house where he died.

Remember now?'

' 'Fraid not, Marshal. Where is this all leading?'

Adam lost his temper. 'Come on, Kember. You

know what I'm talking about. You were the one who sat there on your horse and boasted how you weren't going to be told where to go or what to do by some small-town lawman. You let the whole town know who you were. You killed my father, Kember. And I'm here to make you pay.'

Strangely, Hal Kember seemed almost unmoved by Adam's outburst. Instead he sat there, expressionless. Eventually, he said, 'Sorry to disappoint you, young feller, but you're on the wrong track. I've never been to this . . . this Crawford Gap. When did all this happen?'

'Don't lie, Kember. The whole town knows it was you. I came here to call you out. To give you a better chance than you gave my father—'

Kember was defiant. 'When? I asked you when I did this?'

'I was just seventeen years old. My brother Tom was twelve. The killing broke my mother's heart and for six years she lived like a recluse until she eventually took the fever and died. You ruined my family, Kember, and now I'm going to ruin yours. I can't kill you, but I can ruin your life. You'll never be a congressman, not while I have the breath to speak out.'

Kember suddenly lost his temper. 'I said *tell* me. Tell me when this was!'

'Six years ago. August sixty-eight. Don't tell me

you can't remember that night.'

Kember visibly relaxed. 'Like I told you, Marshal, I was never in Crawford Gap. I've done lots of things I'm not proud of, but killing your pa isn't one of them.'

Kember shuffled in his chair and smiled sardonically.

'You will be too young to remember much of the war, Mr Wade, but as you can see I'm evidence that it left its mark on a lot of people – good and bad. I don't know, maybe this was all I deserved for riding with a man like William Quantrill.'

Adam hid his surprise. He had heard of Quantrill and many of the men who had ridden with him. Partisan rangers they had called themselves as though that gave them an air of official respectability. In fact, according to his father, they were little better than outlaws making the most of other folks' suffering. Some of the men who had ridden with him had become infamous – Cole Younger, the James Brothers and Bloody Bill Anderson were among the most notorious names that his father had told him about. But Hal Kember had not been on that list of badmen.

'August sixty-three, Mr Wade. A whole five years before your father was killed. I was among Quantrill's men when we rode in on Lawrence, Kansas. It was, in the end, a pointless killing spree on a defenceless town. It was just a pillaging of innocent folk. Some escaped, some hid away but it got me to thinking. One of those things I'm not proud of. Was I just another outlaw making the most of poor folks' misfortunes?' He paused briefly and then added, 'Even then, you see, I did have a conscience.

'After Lawrence we attacked a garrison at Baxter Springs and then we wiped out a federal wagon train – caught them by surprise. Guess I must have been our only casualty in the whole shooting. A stray bullet in the back. And for what? What does it all mean now?

'They got me patched up but, well, as you can see for yourself, you can't put back what isn't there anymore. I haven't walked since.'

He paused again, this time to light a cigar, before adding, 'So you see, I couldn't have been in this Crawford Gap in sixty-eight. I was more likely sat here on this balcony watching the sun go down.'

Adam listened but did he believe any of it?

He remembered the night as though it was yesterday. He could still hear his father saying that he had spoken to a man called Kember and with any luck 'they would all calm down'.

His shoulders sagged. Could this be true? Could Kember be the wrong man? If what he was saying was the truth – that he had been chairbound since the infamous Lawrence Massacre – then whoever had killed his father was as far away as ever.

But what about the newspaper story in the *Crawford Announcer*? And the photograph? Adam looked closely at the man in the wheelchair. It was true he did not look much like the man in the newspaper office but pictures were not reliable. And it could have been several years old. Hair turned grey; people put on weight; faces became lined and aged. No, he was sure – this was the man in the long black coat who had dragged his father through the street. He was sure of it . . . or was he? Kember had cast doubts. Either it was a desperate attempt to defend himself or he was telling the truth.

The silence was broken when Kember said, 'Sorry to disappoint you, but like I said, I'm not the man you're looking for: I didn't kill your father.'

Six years. Adam's heart sank. After six years he was still no closer to finding the man who had destroyed his family – killed his father, broken his mother's heart and sent his younger brother on the path to a lawless future – now a wanted man with a price on his head.

'You say this happened in sixty-eight?' Kember asked, and when Adam nodded confirmation, he went on, 'Maybe I can help you. I was running cattle up through Kansas and Missouri in those days. But I had a trail boss – maybe he would know something about it.'

Adam said nothing. He was barely listening as the rancher recalled his early days as a cattleman.

It was then that Adam heard something else – the sound of an approaching rider. Adam rose from his seat and headed for the door, half-hoping that it would be Luke.

Despite his injuries, Adam was ready to take out his bitter disappointment on somebody and right now the younger Kember would provide the perfect victim for all the hate that had built up over the years.

But the newcomer was not Luke Kember: it was Laura Kember.

Hal went through the formalities of introductions before Adam tried to dodge an awkward situation.

'We've met before. I've rented a room at the – er – your hotel.' Smiling coyly, Laura held out her hand. 'We haven't officially met, Mr Wade. What are you doing out this way?'

Was there something hidden in that question? He had told her that he had some unfinished business, but he had said nothing about calling on Kember and son.

'I was hoping Mr Kember might have seen or heard something about those stage robbers or our missing doctor. Far as I know the sheriff's had no luck yet.'

It was a perfectly valid reason for a deputy marshal to call on the biggest rancher in the territory, but he knew that Laura was not convinced. If it had been that simple he would have mentioned it.

But she said nothing, turning instead to lean over and kiss her husband lightly on the cheek. He gripped her arm and held her there longer than she wanted to be, but when he released her she smiled pleasantly.

Was this show of affection for Adam's benefit?

'I called by to see if there's anything you need, Hal.' Then, turning to Adam she added, 'We don't see much of each other, you understand, with me running the hotel while Hal takes care of the ranch and runs for Congress.'

So it was a cover up. The small talk continued for several minutes during which Adam tried to assess the Kembers' domestic situation. Did they have an arrangement? Did Hal, chairbound for almost twelve years and unable to satisfy her needs, know that his young wife – there was about twenty years between them, Adam guessed – would be getting her pleasures somewhere else? And if he didn't know, how would he react if he discovered that his wife's sexual appetite was currently being sated by a visiting deputy US marshal.

Adam wondered if her husband did know, but as long as she was discreet then he was prepared to overlook it. He would need her around to display as a prize wife at the right times. A wheelchair-bound candidate – even a local hero of the Civil War – needed all the help he could get and an attractive young wife was sure to win a few votes from admiring young men.

On those occasions the ogling of strangers would suit Kember; at other times he would be forced to turn a blind eye. But Adam wondered how Kember would react if he ever discovered the truth. A beating like the one Adam had suffered two nights before?

He certainly had the ranch hands willing enough to carry out that sort of punishment.

It was only when Laura unexpectedly left the room that Adam was able to return to the real reason for his visit to the Kember spread.

'You were saying something about a trail boss?' he prompted.

'Sure, can't say he'll be much help though. My man back in those days is now a neighbour of mine: Joe Duggan.'

CHAPTER EIGHT

Duggan waited for the raised voices to calm down. Jess and Brock had been arguing for almost an hour, with an occasional interruption from the young kid, and Duggan had listened from outside as the argument flowed first one way then the other. There were long silences, inevitably broken by Jess's insistence that they should leave right away, collect their loot and head for the state border. But Sam Brock remained unconvinced. The kid wasn't fit for a long ride – at this the injured member of the trio registered his own protest – and if Jess wanted to leave he knew the way.

And so it went on . . . first Brock winning and then Jess.

As he stood in the shade of the veranda and eavesdropped on the conversation, Joe Duggan's head filled with all sorts of questions. Why was Sam Brock being so stubborn in his insistence that the three men stayed on the ranch instead of putting a distance between themselves and the law? Now that the kid was fit to ride there was nothing to keep them there, unless ... was Sam about to demand some sort of payment for his years of silence? Hadn't the information about the rail workers' payroll repaid any debt Joe owed? It was easy pickings – raiding a poorly guarded stage on a quiet trail into town.

It had not been his fault that the kid had been wounded.

All thoughts of Brock and his reasons for delaying his departure from the Double D were interrupted by a new outbreak of raised voices from inside the house. Moments later Jess came running down the steps. He was in a fury.

'Crazy stubborn bastard!' he snarled, as he hurried past Duggan towards his horse hitched at a rail near the side of the house. The rancher stood and watched as Jess quickly saddled up and, digging his heels viciously into the side of the stallion, rode off at a gallop.

'He'll be back when he cools down.'

Duggan had not heard the approaching footsteps and he turned abruptly to face Sam Brock.

'What's eating him?'

For an answer, Brock put his arm around the other's shoulder – a gesture that to any onlooker would have suggested a token of close friendship.

Duggan knew there was a different reason.

'I think with Jess out there sulking and the kid resting it's time we had that talk,' said Brock quietly. Duggan could only guess what was coming.

It was late afternoon, darkness approaching, on a hot, still day when they finally got the herd to settle down on the edge of the small, stopover town.

In six, maybe seven days they would reach the rail depot; the cattle would be loaded and headed for the Eastern city markets and eventually on to the fine tables of the finest restaurants, and the men would be free to go their own way. But that was maybe a week or so away and it had been a long, hard drive from the Big K and the men had been growing restless. There had been bickering, a few fights that made a mockery of the renowned comradeship among cattlemen, and a general dissatisfaction at the endless supply of chuck wagon beans. The men needed a break before things got out of hand altogether so Sam Brock had ridden into the little town and reported back to the trail boss.

'There's a saloon, a couple of eating places and a bathhouse. And a whorehouse. The townsfolk are used to cattle drovers having their fun.'

'That's all we'll need,' Duggan grinned, leaving Brock to organize the unlucky group to stay behind and tend the herd.

An hour later the cowboys from the Big K rode into the little town of Crawford Gap and many lives were changed for ever. . . .

All had been going well. Joe was filling himself with drink at the card table and the woman on his lap helped to decorate the gloomy saloon. But then came the first shot. . . .

It was fired at the swinging sign over the barber shop. Then another smashed a store window.

Within minutes, two of the cowboys were drunkenly trying to encourage locals to share their bottle of cheap whiskey.

Inside the saloon, Joe Duggan was enjoying a string of winning hands at the poker table. And with each hand came an extra slug of whiskey. Duggan was Hal Kember's trail boss and for years he had been the wheelchair-bound rancher's right-hand man. And a good friend. But not tonight.

Tonight he had decided to free himself of all responsibility for 1800 head of prime Texas beef. He had got them through the stampede with the loss of only a few longhorns; he had kept men and herd happy for twelve long weeks since leaving the Big K. And above all he had ignored the bottle in his saddle-bag.

Sam Brock lounged at the bar and toyed with his beer glass but he kept a close watch on his boss. He knew Duggan of old. He was a man with a short fuse that needed only the slightest spark to ignite. And that spark *usually came out of a bottle. Brock also guessed, rightly, that if Hal Kember had known of Duggan's weakness for strong liquor his days as a trail boss would be over. And that would be the cue for Sam Brock to step in and to hell with a long-standing friendship.*

Watching over a herd at night was best done by a cowboy who drank nothing stronger than creek water and although he was now enjoying a beer, Brock, unlike Duggan, could handle a few weeks away from a whiskey glass.

He turned his attention away from the card table as a saloon girl brushed his shoulder. Duggan could take care of himself for the next hour or two. . . .

Later, after paying off the woman, Brock returned downstairs to find the trail boss in a filthy mood. He had lost more than he had won at the card table and had clearly drunk more than he could hold. It was then that one of the drink-fuelled cowboys came staggering in off the street and across to the table where Duggan was involved in a heated argument over a deal.

'Hey, Joe, lawman's on his way,' the newcomer slurred. 'Figure he's lookin' for trouble.'

Duggan kicked away his chair and hitched his gunbelt. 'Then I'm ready for him.'

It was then that Brock stepped in.

'Easy, Joe, the sheriff's only doin' his job. Prob'ly just wants to talk.'

Duggan said nothing but smiled as he shook off Brock's

restraining hand. He went outside just as the lawman was reaching the saloon. Brock lit his cigar and joined his boss, following closely behind as he stepped out on to the boardwalk.

It was then that he knew the night was going to turn sour – the moment when Duggan had squared up to the lawman and announced, 'That's me – this is Hal Kember's outfit.'

As Brock stood and watched the two men he prepared himself for trouble ahead. When the sheriff addressed Joe as Mr Kember and the other didn't put him straight, that was the sign that things would only get worse.

The sheriff's friendly warning about keeping the peace lasted for an hour but it was close on eleven o'clock when the whiskey got the better of Joe Duggan. Drunk and running out of control, he left the saloon. Barking orders to his drunken men, he mounted his horse and headed for the house at the end of the street – the sheriff's house. Nobody tried to stop him and within minutes they were all looking on in horror as the helpless peace officer was dragged through the street of his town and left to die in front of his grieving family.

It was Brock and two young drovers who eventually dragged Duggan away and out of town. And it was Brock who sat around the dying embers of a fire and listened while a seriously drunk trail boss spilled his guts. Almost dismissing the death of the Crawford Gap lawman as a casualty of a cowhands' night out, Duggan unburdened

124

himself of another confession that Brock could keep stored for use later. Six years later.

The two riders dismounted and led their horses to drink at the creek. Adam Wade mopped the sweat from his brow while his companion, Sheriff Naylor, lit another cheroot.

The two men had spent much of the hot day searching the miles around the town of Virtue but they were growing increasingly pessimistic and dispirited. So far there had been no signs of the whereabouts of the missing doctor or any trail to follow in the hunt for the stage robbers. Adam was still convinced that Duggan had been lying about seeing the fugitives – it was the only way he could have known that there were three of them – but, short of forcing their way into the Duggan house at gunpoint, there was little they could do. Now the lawmen both knew that with every passing hour the chance of tracking down either the doc or the stage robbers was disappearing.

They were both tired after the day's fruitless search and now the storm clouds were gathering.

The first heavy drops of rain soon followed and with the wind rising both men agreed that it was time to call off the search for the day at least. As the storm's strength increased, the first priority, before the long ride back to town, was to find shelter.

It came in the form of an old rundown shack, hidden away deep in the bushes leading out of the Double D. Darkness was falling as the two men, already soaked through, found some cover for their mounts and then headed for the shelter of the cabin.

The one-roomed building, already in semi-darkness when Adam and Naylor closed the door on the raging storm, was welcoming only as a refuge from the battering weather.

It was cold, wet and sparsely furnished with broken chair, table, pot-bellied stove and a small bed in the far corner, a fireplace that had not been used in a long time. An oil lamp stood on the mantel.

The windows were boarded up and there was a back door. Adam lit the oil lamp and examined the interior of the shack. It took him less than a minute to spot it – the crumpled bunk in the corner of the room was stained . . . with blood.

'Sheriff,' he said, waving Naylor over. 'What do you make of this?'

Naylor rubbed his finger over the patch of deepening red.

'Recent, I'd say.' And then, 'What's this?' He reached behind the pillow and pulled out a blood-stained doctor's knife. A further search of the area around the bed revealed several swabs. And a stethoscope. 'So the doc was here. And so was the man he was taken out of town to tend.'

'Where does this get us?' Naylor asked, after the two men had looked in vain for more evidence of the doctor's presence.

'It leads us back to Duggan,' Adam said firmly. 'And if I'm right that's where we'll find the stage robbers. They're not long gone, Sheriff, they are holed up somewhere on Double D land.

'I think we should head back to town and you can get your posse together again. This time I've a feeling you won't be going home empty-handed.'

Duggan lay in his bunk, staring at the ceiling unable to sleep but seeing nothing.

He knew that the day would eventually come when he would have to face up to his past; when somebody from that past – it was Sam Brock – would turn up and demand a price for his long silence.

Why did it happen? Why had that brainless town sheriff challenged him? They had said the town – what was it called, Crawford Gap? – was used to trail-herds having a good time. If he had stayed out of it, the sheriff could have enjoyed a quiet old age. Instead ... it was the whiskey, of course. It had always been the whiskey. Damn fool of a sheriff shouldn't have challenged him. If he hadn't the rest wouldn't have come out either.

He didn't remember too much about the night, not even now when Brock was there to remind him.

What had made him use Hal Kember's name? Perhaps the past was catching up with him; perhaps the whiskey had muddled his thinking again. Why else would he have confessed to Brock that it was not a Yankee bullet that Kember had caught in the back, but a stray from Duggan's own rifle. A shot fired in panic.

They had been coming under attack from the local farmers and the bullets were flying everywhere. There was no safe ground.

Now Brock wanted paying for keeping the information away from Hal Kember.

'I'm sick of running from the law,' he had said, as the two men sat on the porch and listed to the rain rattling against the roof of the house. 'It's time I did something other than raid banks and hold up stages. I have a hankering for some ranching, Joe. I think it's time we became partners.'

Duggan turned over and sat up on his bunk as he tried to take in Brock's demand: to keep silent about the killing of the Crawford Gap lawman and the shooting – accident though it was – that had put Hal Kember in a wheelchair, Brock wanted a share of the Double D. The idea of sharing his ranch with a man like Brock sickened Duggan, and the threat would always be there. He would never be free.

Duggan strolled across the darkened room and gazed out at the driving rain. His mind was in turmoil. He had plenty of thinking to do before he agreed to the demand. Sam Brock was a bank robber and probably a murderer being hunted by the local sheriff and, as a partner, Duggan knew he couldn't be trusted.

But what was the alternative? Could he turn an old friend – especially one who knew far too much and was prepare to use it – in to the law? And could he do that without Sam Brock's discovering that he had been betrayed?

He was still pondering when he eventually returned to his bunk and made another effort to sleep.

For the second night in succession, Sam Brock waited until the house was in total darkness before saddling up and leading his horse a safe distance, then mounting up and heading away from the ranch.

Jess Archer cursed and spat. He had ridden out of the Double D with one intention. He was sick of Brock's decision-making, looking after that kid as though he was his own flesh and blood instead of just another trigger-happy young buck who had joined up with them only a few weeks ago. The raid on the stage was only his second job and he had gone and got himself shot up. Brock had hidden the heavy strong-box because the kid was not fit enough to ride; now he was and still Sam was refusing to leave the Double D.

Well, it was time for Jess to take action of his own. He was sick of all this waiting around. Ever since his latest run-in with big Sam that afternoon he had thought of only one thing – getting his money and hightailing it out of there.

But now, as the rain and wind lashed and he had trouble keeping his feet in the darkness, things were not so simple. He was sure he had come to the right place. Even in the darkness he remembered the landmarks of the rise to the hiding place in the rocks.

Shielding his eyes against the driving rain, Jess searched the scrub and crevices between the rocks without any luck. Baffled, he tried to recall the route they had taken after the hold-up.

They had ridden up to the top of the ridge and halfway down the other side to where he was now searching. But there was no sign of the box. He cursed again and took out his frustration by kicking out aimlessly.

With the wind and rain showing no signs of easing and Jess's mind on other things, he did not hear the rider's approach. As he reluctantly decided to abandon his search he turned to see the shadowy but familiar figure stepping out of the darkness. Silhouetted against the leaden night sky was the last man he wished to see out there in the storm.

Startled, he rose to his full height as the newcomer dismounted.

Jess Archer froze as the man in the shadows unholstered his gun.

'Sam! What—?

'Evenin', Jess. Didn't think you would be too hard to find.'

'Listen Sam,' Jess tried playing for time, 'I know how this looks. I just wanted to check that the box was still here.'

Brook chuckled. 'And it isn't, is it? So let me tell you how it looks.' He sneered. 'It looks to me like you're running out on us, Jess. That you thought you'd come here, pick up the box and then head on out with all our money.'

'No, Sam, I—'

He stepped backwards, slipping on to his back.

Brock remained calm.

'You know, Jess, one thing I've always asked from anybody who rides with me is loyalty. Be loyal to me and I'll be loyal back. That's the rule. You just have to ask Joe Duggan. He'll tell you; he knows all about loyalty. If you can't trust people to be loyal, then what've you got?'

Jess was starting to worry. He hadn't expected this. The plan had been simple enough; shoot open the box, and unload the cash and head for the border. To hell with Brock and the kid. If they wanted to hang around and wait for a lynch mob they were welcome to it. He had to get out.

He stayed silent but started to edge back into the darkness. The Colt was still aimed steadily at his chest. Brock was too calm. He should have been angry, shouting. Not like this. Not calm. He scrambled to his feet.

'What you gonna do, Sam?'

Brock's cold stare gave no hint. Instead he said simply, 'This.'

The first bullet hit Jess full in the chest; the second in the stomach; the third in the shoulder.

The scream rose above the howl of the wind as the dying man fell backwards, trying desperately to clutch at a nearby bush as he toppled over and into the shrub below.

Brock reholstered his gun, walked forward and peered into the darkness.

'Loyalty, Jess,' he said quietly. 'Not too much to ask.'

It was an hour before dawn when the rain eventually eased and Adam and Naylor rode back into

Virtue. The town slept – even the saloon was in darkness – when their horses splashed through the flooded street.

'We'll catch an hour's sleep and then I'll round up a few men to go search for the doc,' the sheriff suggested.

Then, after a pause he added, 'More likely it's his body we'll be bringing in.'

The two men had spent the time sheltering in the shack trying to piece together the events since the stage robbery.

'The way I see it is this,' Adam said. 'One of the killers had been shot in the chest – we know that much – so he would need a doctor. Then, two others came in to town and either persuaded McLaine to go with them or, more likely, forced him.

'They took him to this shack where he patched up the wounded man and then. . . .'

His voice petered out leaving Naylor to add his own finish, 'They killed the doc and got rid of the body, burying it somewhere in the undergrowth.'

Adam nodded.

'But why did they stay behind? They could have been out of the state and well on the way to their next job before we got anywhere near them.'

'Not with a wounded man and a heavy strong-box,' Adam argued.

'My guess is that they hid the box somewhere up in the hills, ready for when they were all fit to ride.'

Naylor emitted a snort of sarcasm. 'Loyalty among thieves, you reckon. 'Sides, they couldn't do that without help.' He paused then added, 'And you think—'

'Duggan. It has to be him. He knew there were three of them. How – unless he had seen them himself? And was helping them?'

The sheriff said nothing. Adam still hadn't told him of that night six years ago when he had seen his father dragged to his death by a man who said his name was Hal Kember. And that man, Adam now believed, was Joe Duggan.

Back at his hotel room, Adam bathed his bruised face, tried to restrap his tender ribs and prepared for what lay ahead. He had no idea then that the face-to-face with his father's killer would not bring an end to his quest for revenge. Instead it would lead to another conflict but this time there would be no winner.

CHAPTER NINE

Luke Kember woke early but in truth he had slept little during the night. He had had other things on his mind; the driving rain had kept him awake, offering all the time he needed to think through his next move. Eavesdropping on his father's private conversations was nothing new for young Luke: he needed to know what was going on at the Big K for use when he eventually took over from the old man.

That couldn't come a day too soon. His father had gone soft in his old age. Maybe it was because he was stuck in that wheelchair; maybe it was because that cow of a wife he'd married had him wrapped around her little finger. Maybe he just didn't have the heart to run the place like he used to. And now he was hankering for a political career. He had even hinted that his old friend Duggan might be the man to take over. Luke wasn't going to let that happen.

But it was the woman who worried him most. She had only to link up with the wrong man and the ranch would be hers.

Did the old man really think that she was living the life of a nun in that hotel? If so, he was crazy, but at least Luke could happily keep him in ignorance by making the woman pay for his silence.

As he stood and watched the rain lashing down he thought about the latest on her list of bedmates . . . that deputy marshal Wade. With the help of his drink-fuelled ranch hands he'd given the bastard a good whipping and kicking.

It may have paid him back for that humiliation over the horse, but it hadn't scared him off. Now he was back looking for more.

Luke and his father had been arguing again and he had stormed out leaving the old man to negotiate his chair back into the house. Fuming, his first inclination was to ride off and get drunk; get into a poker game; maybe pick up that slut from the general store he had had his eye on. But he did none of these things. Instead he decided to stay behind and try to persuade the old man that he seriously needed that money to pay off his debts. What was a few hundred to a man like Hal Kember?

Regaining his temper after the earlier outburst, he had been about to approach his father again when he heard a familiar voice. The man Wade was in the house and he was arguing with the old man. Luke slid behind the pillar that formed part of the partition that separated two of the main rooms and listened as Wade and Kember raised their voices in disagreement. Catching only parts of the heated conversation Luke managed to put together enough information to form the next part of his plan to get Wade out of his hair.

Joe Duggan had to be told that Adam Wade was about to call on him. And if Luke read the mood right, he guessed Wade would be looking for trouble. Let Duggan deal with the meddling marshal.

Now, as the night rain eased, Luke left the house and headed for the Double D Ranch.

Joe Duggan listened without interrupting while Kember's son related what he had overheard. A marshal was coming and there was little doubt that he would be in the company of the sheriff and a posse. This was not his fight. It had no connection with that night in Crawford Gap, or the stray bullet that had made Kember a chair-bound cripple. They were looking for Sam Brock and the rest of the stage robbers. Where was he? And where was that sneering snake Jess? He hadn't seen either of them since yesterday when Jess had ridden off in a state of fury after a blazing row with Sam. Maybe Brock had gone after him, to calm him down and bring him back. But Duggan didn't want him back. None of them. Upstairs the kid's wounds were healing quickly. He was fit to ride out. And Sam's grand idea of settling down to a share in the Double D – that wasn't going to happen.

'Thought I ought to warn you, Joe,' Luke finished, watching Duggan for some sort of reaction to the news that he was on a marshal's wanted list even though he did not know why.

Duggan hardly seemed to be listening. 'Fine, kid, so you warned me. Now get back to your own ground – I need time to think.'

Ungrateful bastard, Luke thought, but said, 'I rode out here to lend a hand, Joe, I think I'll stick around.'

'Please yourself. Meantime, I've got business to tend to.' He walked off leaving Luke to wonder why he had bothered to ride over.

The sun was climbing into a cloudless sky after the night storm.

'Good day for a showdown,' Luke reflected, as he watched Duggan enter the house.

He was still standing near the house when a lone rider appeared over the hill, rode in at a gentle trot, pulled his horse to a halt outside the main house and, without a word, went in.

Sam Brock had returned.

*

In Virtue, Sheriff Jack Naylor was having no luck rounding up a second posse. The men who had ridden with him two days earlier had lost the will to search for the stage robbers, believing them to be long gone from the area. So, when Adam staggered, bleary-eyed out of his hotel and across to the sheriff's office he found Naylor sitting alone behind the desk.

'I guess this is where we get to earn our money,' the sheriff grinned, as the other man arrived. 'At least you're looking a bit healthier.'

It was true. The bruises and cuts were slowly healing and the ache in his ribs was easing. When he stretched the pain was at least bearable. 'Just be sure your gun hand is in order,' Naylor added gloomily. 'My guess is you're gonna need it.'

An hour later four men rode away from the sheriff's office and headed for the Double D. Ed Hanley, who had been Naylor's deputy until a better job came along with the stage company, had volunteered.

He had known the murdered company man and catching the killers was more of a personal mission than a job on the posse line.

Cabe Hackett was going along on the ride for a far different reason. He was on a long losing run at the card tables and he badly needed a share of the reward money. And he had always fancied himself behind a gun. Adam remembered him from the day he first arrived in Virtue, the morning when he had stopped him putting a bullet in the back of Luke Kember.

This time Hackett was still sober so early in the morning, but Naylor had to remind him that there would be no gunplay without his say-so.

'I'll do what I have to do,' Hackett snapped. 'You can count on me, Sheriff.'

Naylor might have taken that at face value, but Adam was far from sure. Hackett wasn't the sort of man he'd like to have around in a crisis.

As the four riders approached the Double D, Naylor ordered them all to dismount.

'I'll go in alone and talk to Duggan,' the sheriff said. 'I know him: if those three are hiding out at his place it will be because he's threatened.'

Hackett snarled, 'It's your hide you're risking, Sheriff, but if you ask me we should all go in together.'

'Well, I ain't asking you, Cabe. You wait here with Ed and the marshal.'

He remounted and turned to Adam. 'If I'm not back in an hour, the rest is up to you.' He dug his heels into his horse and was off, leaving Adam to wonder what was lying in store.

'Get rid of him, Joe. And make it good.'

Sam Brock was standing behind Duggan as the approaching sheriff pulled his mount to a stop at the hitch rail. There was menace in his voice and the owner of the Double D knew that there was nothing idle about the implied threat.

'Remember, I'm back here, and I'm listening to every word you say,' added Brock, slipping into the background as Duggan went out to greet his visitor. He tried to put on a friendly face.

'Jack, what brings you back here? I thought we'd done our business.'

Naylor studied the other man closely. He seemed to be on edge, nervous, almost as though he was trying to hide something.

'We had, Joe, but now I think those stage robbers are still somewhere around here. One of them was shot up and it looks as though he was treated in one of your shacks.'

There was that nervous look again.

'I thought you'd looked everywhere but if you want to try again, be my guest.'

It was then that Naylor pushed his luck.

'We haven't searched the house.'

Duggan tensed visibly. 'The house? You can't think they'd be holed up in there without me knowing? And Katy – what about her? She'd have seen something. Nothing gets past her.'

Naylor said nothing and Duggan blustered on, 'You think I'm hiding them? Is that it? Why would I? Are you crazy?'

'Maybe,' said Naylor softly. 'Then again . . .' His voice tailed off. 'You won't mind if we have a look round?'

'We? You and who else?'

'I've got men waiting out at the gate. Does that make you nervous, Joe? I thought I'd come in and see you first. Give you a chance to tell me if you know anything, if you've seen anything.'

'Well I ain't seen anything, Sheriff, but if you want to go and get your men I can't stop you looking around.'

'Fine, Joe. I'll be back.'

From his vantage point in the shadows, Brock watched the lawman walking back to his horse. Then, as the sheriff rode off, Duggan turned and hurried inside. He could hardly wait to seize this chance to tell Sam that he had to get out. Pronto.

'Did you convince him?' Brock asked.

'You and the kid have to move out of here,' Duggan warned him. 'He'll be back. And he ain't alone. He knows something.'

Brock cursed. This was not part of his plan for a quiet life running a ranch.

Even though the sheriff had no proof of the identity of the stage robbers, Brock knew from experience that he wouldn't need it.

He and his men wanted somebody and they would shoot first and ask questions later.

They could stay and bluff it out. There had been three men involved in the robbery and shooting and now, with Jess rotting away in the hills, there was only Brock and the kid left.

That damned kid. He'd got under Brock's skin ever since he rode into their camp late one night and invited himself to join them. Sam had admired his nerve. He reminded him of somebody he had known years ago: himself.

Jess hadn't liked the idea, but Brock figured that three guns were better than two when it came to the bigger jobs. Most were easy enough but stages and trains needed extra hands. And the kid was confident. And he was good with a gun.

On the third night the kid had saved his life so he owed him. It had only been a small-town bank but one of the tellers had tried to make a name for himself and made a play for his gun. The kid, already loaded up with cash bags, swung one of them across the head of the would-be hero and sent him crashing across the room. The man's gun had been pointed at Sam's back.

Loyalty, as he had told Jess, meant a lot. But he either didn't care or didn't want to understand. Pity. It had cost him his life.

Now it was Duggan's turn to show some loyalty for six years of silence.

Brock thought for a moment and then said, 'We

ain't running, Joe. Not this time. Not ever again. We need a place to hide out – me and the kid.' Duggan started to interrupt but he was cut short by Brock's cold stare.

'There has to be somewhere on the ranch we can go. Then, in a few days when we show up again you can pass us off as new hands, someone you knew in the old days.'

Joe Duggan knew that any more argument was useless. Already he could sense that the few ranch hands who had seen the strangers were starting to ask questions.

'Where is the one place they won't look?' said Brock, as if thinking aloud. Then, 'The shack. They've already been there, they won't go back.'

Suddenly Brock was in a hurry. 'I'll get the kid. We'll ride out and nobody will know we've been here. I'm counting on you, Joe.'

What choice did Duggan have? The sooner Brock and the kid were gone the better, but could he persuade the sheriff that he knew nothing about the fugitives. Or, the more he thought about it, did he need to? What if. . . ? An alternative plan was forming in Duggan's mind as Brock and the kid came rushing down the staircase.

'Right, Joe. If they get us, then they get you. Remember what's at stake here,' said Brock, the threat left lingering.

The two men hurried out and headed for the barn where their horses were hidden away.

Duggan thought about that. He knew well enough what was at stake and he also knew that Brock and the kid were better dead than alive as far as he was concerned.

He was suddenly aware that Katy was standing at his shoulder.

'Is that the last we'll see of them, Joe?' she asked hopefully.

He put his arm around her. 'Maybe. Just maybe. That'll be up to the sheriff when he comes back.'

Inside the hideaway shack Sam Brock considered the situation. If Duggan did as he had been told there would be no trouble: the sheriff would look somewhere else or, more likely, give up altogether assuming that the stage robbers were well out of the district and heading over the border.

If not. . . .

'Listen, kid,' he said, putting his arm around the shoulder of the younger man as he poured a warming coffee. 'There's something you ought to know about Joe Duggan. It may come in useful one day. . . .'

Duggan waited as the four riders approached around the bend leading up to the house. The sheriff and his marshal friend led the way with two other men bringing up the rear.

Cabe Hackett was one – a vicious, unbalanced drunk, Duggan knew, a man the sheriff wouldn't have within a mile of him by choice. The other, Duggan remembered as a one-time deputy, some-time ranch hand, Ed Hanley, who liked the money more than the work.

As they rode up Joe went inside, strapped on his gunbelt and was back on the ranch-house veranda as the sheriff and his men dismounted. Naylor strode forward, a determined stride that told Duggan that it was time to make his play.

'Joe? You got something to tell us?'

Duggan had already decided that his best chance of seeing through his problem was by having the law on his side. If that meant Sam Brock and the kid getting themselves killed then all the better.

There would be nobody left to bring up the past.

'I couldn't tell you before, Jack. Not with a couple of guns pointed at the back of my head.'

'The way you talk that means you can tell me now,' Naylor snapped. 'Where are they?'

'I'll take you there, Sheriff, but I'm warning you: they're desperate – they won't be taken alive. You're gonna have to shoot it out.'

Naylor grunted. 'That sounds as though you know who they are, Joe.'

'One is Sam Brock – we rode together years back. The other's a kid I don't know. He's the one who got shot in the raid and he's handy with a gun.'

'What about the third man? There was three of them held up the stage.'

'Jess? I ain't seen him since yesterday. He rode off in a rage and never came back. Leastways I ain't seen him since.'

'So, where are they?'

'The shack. The one where you found the doc had been. Brock reckoned you wouldn't go back there.'

Naylor had his doubts. Why was Duggan suddenly being so helpful? 'You gonna help us find this place?'

The rancher nodded. 'Let's go.'

The two men joined the others without noticing the slim figure hidden in the shadows at the side of the house.

Luke Kember smiled to himself. So the stage robbers were hiding out on Double D land. Maybe this was Luke's chance to break away from his Big K ties. The old man had already hinted that Duggan would be taking over the ranch. Or that woman who passed off as his wife. Two birds with one stone. Get rid of Duggan and, if that failed . . . well, Sam Brock would be grateful to know that his friend had betrayed him . . . that he was leading the sheriff and that bastard of a deputy marshal to their hide-out.

Luke knew the layout of the Double D as well as his own. And he knew the shortest route to the shack. He waited until the five riders were out of range, mounted his horse and headed off at full gallop.

He knew he could reach Brock's hide-out ahead of the others.

'Bastard!' Brock cursed. 'I might have known he'd let me down. Always was a coward. Well, at least we know what we're up against. Five of them, you say?'

Luke nodded. His news that Duggan, the sheriff and the others were on their way had hardly surprised Sam. But at least he was now prepared. 'You sticking around, sonny?' he looked at the young Kember.

'The name's Luke and – yeah, I'm sticking around. Looks like you need another gun.'

'Good – that's three against five. And we've got more to fight for than they have. That about evens things up I'd say. Time to arrange a welcome for our visitors. . . .'

CHAPTER TEN

The five dismounted a good distance from the shack and huddled together as Naylor outlined his suggestion for the next step.

'According to Joe, there's just two of them in there – Sam Brock and some gun-happy kid who's been wounded. There may be a third one so we won't be rushing in. I'll call Brock out and we'll see what happens after that. So we spread out and if they don't want to come quiet then we start shooting when I say so.'

Adam interrupted, 'Is there another door out of the place?'

Joe Duggan nodded and signalled towards the back of the building.

'Then I suggest we split up. You and me, Joe, we'll go round the back. The sheriff can take care of this side. We need them alive.'

149

'No we don't,' Hackett snapped. 'If they don't come out hands held high, we don't take no chances.'

The sheriff stepped in. 'We'll do this right and like Cabe says, we shoot if they don't give up, but we need to know where they've stashed the strong-box from the stage.' Then, turning to Adam, he added, 'Don't start shooting until you hear my call.'

'Or they shoot first,' Adam replied. 'Come on, Joe.'

Crouching, the two men hurried through the bushes, circling the shack until they came to a vantage point where the rear door of the cabin was in full view.

They waited until they heard Naylor's voice, loud and demanding.

'You in there! Throw out your guns and follow them, keeping your hands high! We've got the place surrounded.'

They waited.

'Go to hell, Sheriff – and take that lying bastard Duggan with you!'

That was Brock.

A single gunshot was followed by a brief silence. Then Sheriff Naylor called out, 'Don't be a fool. We've got all the time we need. We can stay here all day and night. In the end you'll have to come out peaceful like.' This second warning was followed by another gunshot. Then another. Adam levelled his Winchester and took aim at the small gap in the rotting woodwork near the back door of the cabin. He fired. A yell and a curse from inside was followed by a flurry of shots.

The bullets flew aimlessly into the bushes. Then somebody pushed open the shutter on the window and fired again.

It was Luke Kember.

'What the hell's he got to do with all this?' Adam wondered aloud.

'Dunno,' said Duggan. 'He came to the house to warn me that the sheriff was on his way with a posse. Guess he just changed sides.'

'Bad move,' said Adam, taking aim again and firing at the half-opened window.

From the other side of the shack, the barrage of shooting continued. A scream and another curse suggested that somebody had been hit, but there was no let up until Naylor suddenly emerged from the bushes.

He slumped by Adam's side, gasping for breath.

'One of them's hit – I think it was Brock. If it's bad they'll give up soon enough. I've told the others to hold fire until somebody shows himself.' Suddenly, the rear door of the cabin was pulled open and the third man of the trio – slimmer than the others and quick on his feet even though he appeared to have a serious chest injury – ran into the open, firing wildly as he headed for the cover of the bushes.

Adam froze. His stomach churned.

Then, as Naylor took aim, he leapt forward, knocking the sheriff off his feet and into the bushes.

'Don't shoot,' Adam barked. 'Hold your fire.'

Naylor scrambled to his feet. 'Are you crazy? The kid'll get away.'

'No he won't. And I'm going after him. Alone.'

'Like I said, are you crazy?'

Adam holstered his gun and put his Winchester to one side.

'No, I ain't crazy, Sheriff, and he won't shoot me,' he said quietly. 'He's my brother.'

Tom Wade couldn't believe his eyes. It couldn't be him! Not out here! Leaping into the bushes, he zig-zagged his way out of sight while behind him, the shooting went on. He crouched behind a bush and waited. He disappeared from view briefly. Then Adam called out.

'Tom! Stop! It's me, Adam!'

Crouching, he edged his way into the bushes while behind him the sound of shots appeared to fade into the background.

All at once it was as though the siege at the shack belonged to another time. Another place. Here there were only two men – brothers on opposite sides of the law.

Adam paused and listened. Nothing. Not the sound of distant gunfire. Not even the rustle of leaves.

'Tom?' Adam tried again. And listened. 'Give yourself up. It's your only chance.'

There was another long silence before Tom called out, 'Give myself up? To the hangman? Don't be a fool, Adam. Get out of here. I don't want to hurt you.'

The voice, deeper, stronger, more mature than the last time Adam had heard it, came from behind a clump of bushes to Adam's right. Tom shouted again, 'I think I'll take my chances here.'

Suddenly, he stepped into full view, his sixgun pointed straight at his brother's chest.

'It's been a long time, Adam. Too long. We're not the same people.'

The elder of the Wade brothers who, in their younger days, had shown so much affection for each other, stepped out into the open.

'We're still brothers, Tom. We can work this out and stop it before it's too late.' There was pleading in Adam's voice.

They faced each other in the small clearing. Behind them gunfire went on but neither heard or cared.

Adam nodded towards his younger brother's strapped shoulder.

'Is it bad?' he asked, nodding towards the injury.

'I'll live,' Tom said and laughed. 'Well, maybe. But not long enough to give the hangman his fee.'

'They'll catch you, Tom. Even if I don't take you in. They'll come after you.'

'Take me in? You're not gonna take me in, Adam. Not your own brother.'

'A brother I haven't seen since he ran out. A brother who's on wanted posters throughout the state. Jesus, Tom, what the hell happened to you?'

'Pa got killed, Adam. That's what happened. He got killed doing his job. All lawful. All decent. And all it got him was an early grave. Christ, Adam, you were older; you and Mom – you could handle it. Nobody else cared. Nobody in that stinking little town did anything to find out who did it. I stuck around. Five years. What was left? I had to get out.'

His voice was pleading for understanding but Adam looked at his brother and tried hard to keep the contempt out of his voice.

'And that's your excuse? That's your reason for turning into a thief and a stage robber. . . .'

'And a murderer, Adam. You forgot that.'

'You've killed somebody? Who?'

Tom scoffed. 'I didn't ask their names. But it was them or me. Besides, I didn't get this' – he pointed the gun at his shoulder – 'being the good guy. The stupid stage driver did it. What the hell did the strong-box matter to him?'

'So you killed him?'

'Don't judge me, Adam, not by your standards. Nor by Mom's or Pa's. They ain't me. Anyhow, nobody's taking me in. Not you or anybody, Adam.' He raised his gun and pointed it at his brother again. Adam's hand moved towards his hip fearing that Tom was about to shoot his way out.

But, as he gripped the handle of his Colt, he heard a rustle in the bushes behind him. It was then that Tom fired his six-gun. Twice.

But his brother was not the target.

Adam spun round to see Joe Duggan clutching his chest and falling face down into the dirt. At his side Cabe Hackett also fired – his aim true as Adam turned again to see Tom grasping his stomach and falling in a heap. Hackett fired again.

'No!' Adam screamed, rushing forward to help his stricken brother. As Hackett grinned, enjoying his moment of triumph, Adam knelt down beside his young brother.

'Tom,' he gasped, his voice was no more than a whisper. 'Keep still. Don't try to move. You'll be—'

The wounded brother spluttered, 'Don't say I'll be all right, Adam. I'll be dead in a few minutes. But at least . . . at least I did something . . . good before

they got me . . . That . . . that man I just hit . . . he's
the one who dragged our pa to his death. Brock
told me it was the man Duggan. Killing him, Adam,
ain't that . . . ain't that worth something?'

'Sure, Tom. Sure. It's why I'm here.' But he was
talking to unhearing ears and he was looking into
unseeing eyes. Tom Wade was dead.

CHAPTER ELEVEN

Adam Wade stood over the grave of a member of his family for the third time. First it had been his father, an honest lawman who had been killed in the line of duty. Then it was his mother, a good woman who had died of a fever after years of suffering brought on by a broken heart. Now his young brother Tom was lying in his grave. Bank robber, stage robber and killer. A life destroyed by others like Sam Brock. But was that true? Tom had broken the law and ridden out of Crawford Gap before he had met Brock. His name had been on wanted lists long before the stage robbery. He was a self-confessed murderer who, despite everything, had shown no regret as he lay dying in his brother's arms. Adam offered a silent prayer and then added in hushed voice, 'I let you down, Tom. And I'm sorry. Rest in peace, Brother.'

He replaced his hat, turned away from the graveside

and mounted his horse. It was time to ride back down the hill into Virtue. He had to say his farewells.

Laura Kember greeted him with a smile as he entered the hotel.

'You're moving on?' she asked, as they shared a drink at the bar.

'Soon as I've finished this drink,' Adam answered. 'Brock's in jail and I think your young stepson's learned his lesson. Did I tell you he was found cowering in the corner of the shack? He'd wet himself, poor little brat. Young Luke's all mouth, but I think you already know that, don't you?'

Laura raised her glass and smiled. 'Oh, not all mouth, Marshal. Not at all, as I know well enough since you walked out on me.'

Adam smiled. 'And here was me thinking I was the only one . . . say so long to your husband for me, will you?'

Adam Wade left the bar of the Kember Hotel, mounted his chestnut, swung away from the rail outside and headed back along the trail that would eventually take him back to Crawford Gap.

His life had changed. His family had gone. It was time he thought about his own future.